# THE THREE-YEAR ITCH

It has been three blissful years since Abbie married Grey Lockwood. She has it all: a glamorous jet-setting career, a beautiful home and, best of all, a loving husband to come home to. Her friends tease her that they would never leave a man as devilishly sexy as Grey on his own for long, but she always thought their marriage was based on trust. Yet . . . has she left Grey alone once too often? He no longer seems satisfied with a part-time lover. He wants a full-time wife — *any* wife!

*Books by Liz Fielding*
*in the Linford Romance Library:*

# LIZ FIELDING

---

# THE THREE-YEAR ITCH

*Complete and Unabridged*

# LINFORD
*Leicester*

First published in Great Britain in 1997

First Linford Edition
published 2015

A catalogue record for this book is available
from the British Library.

ISBN 978–1–4448–2477–3

Published by
F. A. Thorpe (Publishing)
Anstey, Leicestershire

Set by Words & Graphics Ltd.
Anstey, Leicestershire
Printed and bound in Great Britain by
T. J. International Ltd., Padstow, Cornwall

This book is printed on acid-free paper

For Jan and Kate,
who know a thing or two about
sheep . . . and slurry

# 1

Abbie Lockwood glanced sympathetically at the crowds milling around the luggage carousel as she walked by, but she didn't stop. She didn't have to. Travelling time was too precious a commodity to be wasted queueing for luggage, and she carried no more than the drip-dry, crumple-free essentials, packed along with her precious laptop computer and camera, in a canvas bag small enough to be carried aboard a plane with her.

She moved swiftly, eagerly through the formalities and into the airport arrival hall, glancing about her for Grey, her excitement deflating just a little as she didn't immediately spot the heart-churning smile that told her he was glad she was home. She stretched slightly onto her toes, although at five feet ten in her drip-dry socks, she didn't really need to. Besides, he wasn't the kind of man you could miss. He stood a head clear of the most pressing crowd and she knew that if she hadn't immediately caught sight of his tall, athletic figure it was because he wasn't there.

Abbie's sharp stab of disappointment punctured her brilliant feeling of elation at being home, at a job well done. Grey always came to meet her. Never failed, no matter how busy he was. Then she shook herself severely. It was ridiculous to be so cast down. He might just have been delayed, or a client might have needed him urgently — he might even be in court. She hadn't been able to contact him directly, so he hadn't been able to explain . . .

He'd probably left a message, she thought, fighting her way through the crowds to the information desk. It was unreasonable to expect him to drop everything and come running just because she had been away for a couple of weeks and was dizzily desperate to hold him in her arms and hug him

2

tight. It was just that he had never failed her before. That was all.

'My name is Abigail Lockwood,' she told the young woman at the desk. 'I was expecting my husband to meet me but he isn't here. I wonder if he left a message for me?'

The girl checked. 'I'm afraid there's nothing here for you, Mrs Lockwood.'

'Oh, well,' she said, trying to hide a sudden tiny tremor of unease, the totally ridiculous feeling that something must be wrong. 'I expect we've got our wires crossed somewhere. I'd better take a taxi.' The girl smiled on automatic; she had clearly heard it all a thousand times before.

\* \* \*

All the excitement, the high of returning home had drained from her by the time the taxi set her down outside the elegant mansion block where she and Grey lived, and she just felt tired. But she found a smile for the porter,

3

who gallantly admired her tan and asked her if she'd had a good trip.

'Fine, thanks, Peter,' she replied. 'But I'm glad to be home.' Two fraught weeks touring the sprawling streets of Karachi with a distraught mother in search of her snatched daughter in a tug-of-love case had not been a barrel of laughs.

'That's just what Mr Lockwood said not five minutes ago, when he got back.'

'He's home?' In the middle of the afternoon? Something must be seriously wrong.

'Yes, Mrs Lockwood, and very glad to see *you* back safe and sound, I'm sure. Leave your bag; I'll bring . . . '

But Abbie, too impatient to wait for the ornate wrought-iron lift to crank her up two floors, was already flying up the stairs, her bag banging against her back, her long legs taking the steps two at a time, all tiredness forgotten in her need for reassurance. Then as she reached the door she felt suddenly quite foolish. If Grey had been ill, or hurt,

Peter would certainly have said something.

It was far more likely that, realising that he wouldn't make the airport in time, Grey had come home to surprise her. Well, she thought, her full mouth lifting into a mischievous little smile, she would surprise him instead. She opened the door quietly, put her bag on the hall floor and for a moment just enjoyed the wonderful sensation of being in her own home, surrounded by the accumulated clutter of their lives, instead of confined to the anonymous comfort of a hotel room.

She could hear sounds of activity coming from the small study that they shared and, easing off her shoes, she padded silently across the hall. Grey was propped on the edge of his desk, listening to the messages on the answering machine, pen poised above his notepad to jot down anything that needed a response.

For a moment she stood in the doorway, simply enjoying the secret pleasure of watching him. She never tired of looking at the way his thick, dark hair curled onto his strong neck, at the sculptured shape of his ear, the long, determined set of his jaw. She could see his beloved face reflected in the glass-fronted bookcase, the furrow of concentration as he noted a telephone number. She was reflected beside him but, head bent over the notepad, he had not yet noticed her.

Then, as he reached her message, telling him the arrival time and flight number of her plane, he swore softly, glanced swiftly at his watch and reached for the phone. As he did so he finally caught sight of her reflection and their eyes met through the glass.

'Abbie!' he exclaimed. 'I'm so sorry! I've only just got your message . . . '

'So I heard,' she said, her soft voice full of mock reproach. 'And since I rang twenty-four hours ago I shall want a detailed itinerary of your movements to cover every last second of that time.' She had been teasing, expecting him to respond in kind, with lurid details of an impossible night of debauchery and an offer to demonstrate . . . Instead he raked his long fingers distractedly through his hair.

'I had to go away for a couple of days. I've only just got back.'

'Oh?' It was odd, she thought; flinging herself into his arms in the frenetic excitement of the arrivals hall at the airport had always seemed the most natural thing in the world, but here, in their own home, the atmosphere was more constrained, with the answering machine droning on the background and Grey poised on the edge of the desk, pen still in his hand. 'And what exotic paradise have you been gadding off to the minute I turn my back?' she asked.

For the space of a moment, no more, his eyes blanked. 'Manchester,' he said. 'A case conference.' If it hadn't been so ridiculous, Abbie would have sworn he'd said the first thing that came into his head, but she had no time to think

7

about it before he dropped the pen and closed the space between them, gathering her into his arms. 'Lord, but I've missed you,' he said.

She couldn't answer, couldn't tell him how much she had missed him, because her mouth was entirely occupied with a long and hungry kiss that scorched her in a way that the Karachi sun had quite failed to do. When finally he lifted his head, his warm brown eyes were creased into a smile. 'Welcome home, Mrs Lockwood.'

'Now that,' she said huskily, 'is what I call a welcome.' Abbie lifted her hands to his face, smoothed out the lines that fanned about his eyes with the tips of her fingers. 'You look tired. I suppose you've been working all the hours in the day, and half the night as well, while I've been away?'

'It helps to pass the time,' he agreed. 'But you're absolutely right. I am tired. So tired, in fact, that I think I shall have to go to bed. Immediately.' Abbie squealed as he swiftly bent and caught her behind the knees, swinging her up into his arms. 'And I'm going to have to insist you come with me. You know how very badly I sleep when I'm on my own.'

'Idiot!' she exclaimed, laughing. 'Put me down this minute. I've been travelling all day, and if I don't have a shower . . . '

'A shower?' Grey came to a sudden halt. Then his mouth curved into a slow smile that was so much more dangerous than his swift grin. 'Now that is a good idea.'

'No, Grey!' she warned him.

He took no notice of her protest, or her ineffectual struggles to free herself from his arms, but headed straight into the bathroom and, stopping only to kick off his shoes, stepped with her into the shower stall.

'No!' Her voice rose to a shriek as the jet of water hit them both. Then he was kissing her hungrily as the water ran over their faces, pulling her close as the water drenched her T-shirt, pouring in

9

warm rivulets between her breasts and across the aching desire of her abdomen. Then she gave a whispered, 'Oh, yes,' as he eased her T-shirt over her head, unfastened her bra and tossed them into a dripping pile upon the bathroom floor.

His lips tormented hers as he hooked his finger under the waistband of her jeans, flicking open the button as with shaking fingers she reached up and began to unfasten his shirt. Then he slipped his hands inside her jeans and over her buttocks, easing them down her legs.

She was almost melting with desire by the time he turned her round and began slowly to stroke shower gel across her shoulders and down her back. A long, delicious quiver of pleasure escaped her lips and he laughed softly. 'I thought you said no,' he murmured, his tongue tracing a delicate little line along the curve of her ear as his hands slid round to cradle her breasts and draw her back against him.

'I'll give you twenty-four hours to stop,' she sighed, lying back against him, relishing the intense pleasure of his wet skin against hers, the touch of his hands stroking the soap over her body. She had dreamed of this in the sterile emptiness of her hotel room five thousand miles away and had determined that, no matter what the temptation, how good the story, she had accepted her last foreign assignment.

It would be a wrench. She loved her job. She was a good photo-journalist and knew the feature on tug-of-love children that she was putting together needed the on-the-spot reality of her Karachi trip. The desperate hunt, the endless knocking on the doors, an officialdom that seemed not to care about a woman deprived of her child, the photographs that would show the anguish when she had finally found her daughter, only to have her snatched from her grasp and bundled away once more, would make a heart-breakingly compelling story.

But no more. Every time she went away it seemed that her marriage suffered just a little. Nothing that she could put her finger on. Tiny irritations. But things happened to them while they were apart that they seemed unable to share. She came back impatient at complaints about a leaky washing machine or some other domestic drama when she had spent a week with refugees or the victims of some terrible natural catastrophe. But Grey was the senior partner in a prestigious law firm. He didn't have time to deal with the minor domestic trivialities of life. He had once joked that they could do with someone else — a job-share wife to take care of the details while she was away.

'I think I'd rather have a job-share husband,' she had returned, easily enough, joining in with his laughter, but the warning had not been lost on her.

Grey Lockwood was the kind of man who turned women's heads. And, like most men, he only had to look helpless and they flocked to mother him. Except that mothering wasn't all they had in mind. She worked very hard to ensure that her absences were as painless as possible, but some things couldn't be foreseen. How long would it be before some sympathetic secretary noticed the vulnerable chink in their marriage and began to lever it apart with personal services that extended beyond the use of her washing machine? Certain as she was that he loved her, she knew Grey was not made of wood. He was a warm, flesh-and-blood man — full of life, full of love. And she loved him as much as life itself.

She turned eagerly in his arms and began to soap him, spreading her hands across his broad shoulders, slipping the tips of her fingers through the coarse dark hair that spread across his chest and arrowed down across his flat belly until she heard him gasp.

'I don't know about you, Grey,' she said, tipping her head back to look at him from beneath the heavy lids of her fine grey eyes, 'but I think I'm clean enough.'

He said nothing, simply flipped the shower switch, pulled a towel from the rack to wrap about her shoulders, then, sweeping her up into his arms, he stepped out of the shower stall and carried her to bed.

The first time after she had been away was always special. A slow rediscovery of one another, a reaffirmation of their love. But now Grey seemed seized by an almost desperate urgency to know her, to reclaim her as his. Even as he followed her down onto the bed she saw something in his face, some savage, primeval need that excited her even as a quiver of apprehension rippled through her.

'Grey?' Her almost tentative query was brushed aside as he reared above her, his knee parting her legs, the dominant male driven by the desire to plant his seed.

She cried out as her breath was driven from her, her hands seizing the

14

muscle-packed flesh of his shoulders, her nails digging in as he took her on a roller-coaster ride of meteoric intensity — a ride which she began as a passenger but then, as the pace, almost the fury of his driving passion set alight a hitherto unsuspected chord of wanton sensuality deep within her, she rose to him, matching his ardour thrust for thrust until they came crashing back to earth, satiated, exhausted, drenched with sweat.

As he rolled away from her and lay staring at the ceiling a long shuddering sigh escaped him. 'You've been away too long, Abbie.' Then he turned to her. 'Did I hurt you?'

She shook her head. 'Surprised me a little, that's all.' She touched the score-marks her nails had riven in his shoulders in the heat of passion. 'But I like surprises.' And she reached forward to lay her lips against the slick salty warmth of his skin, sighing contentedly as he gathered her into his arms.

Tomorrow she would ache a little,

but it would be a good feeling and she would carry it with her as a secret knowledge, a constant reminder of the fact that she was desired, loved.

\* \* \*

Abbie was the first to wake, the weight of Grey's arm across her waist disturbing her as she moved. For a moment she remained perfectly still, soaking in the pleasure of having his face buried against her shoulder, the pleasure of being home. Going away had its miseries, but without separation there would never be these blissful reunions. She lay quietly, her face inches from his, reminding herself of every feature, every tiny line that life had bestowed upon him, very gently touching an old childhood scar above his brow.

She could tell the exact moment when he woke. He didn't move, didn't open his eyes. There was just the faintest change in breathing, the tiniest contraction of the muscles about his eyes. She grinned. It was an old game, this.

How long could he maintain the pretence? She began slowly to trace the outline of his face with the tip of one finger, moving slowly up the darkening shadow of his chin to his lower lip. Did it quiver slightly under the lightest teasing of her nail? She gave him the benefit of the doubt; this was not a game to be hurried. She dipped her head to trail a tiny tattoo of kisses across his throat, his chest, her tongue flickering across flat male nipples that leapt to attention.

Still he did not move, and she continued her teasing quest across the hard, flat plane of his stomach until the tell-tale stirring of his manhood could no longer be ignored. But, before she had quite registered the fact that the game was over and won, he had turned, flipping her over onto her back, his hands on her wrists, holding her arms above her head, pinning her to the bed, utterly at his mercy. 'So, you want to play games, do you, Mrs Lockwood?'

She lowered her lashes seductively. 'Why, sir, I don't know what you mean.'

'Then I'll have to show — ' The telephone began to ring. For a moment Grey gazed down at her, then he dropped the briefest kiss on her mouth. 'It appears that you have a reprieve.' He released her, rolling away and rising to his feet in one smooth movement.

She didn't want a reprieve and reached out for him. 'Whoever it is will leave a message, Grey. Don't go.'

'It'll be Robert. I should have phoned him an hour ago.' He raised her hand absently to his lips. 'Why don't you go and see if you can rustle up something for supper?'

'Well, gee, shucks, thanks, mister,' she murmured as he disappeared in the direction of the study. It was the first time she had ever come *third*. To a phone call and food.

\* \* \*

'Grey?' He lifted his head from his distant contemplation of the supper Abbie had thrown together from the rather sparse contents of the refrigerator. 'Can we talk?'

'Mmm?' He had been distracted ever since he had talked to Robert; now he seemed to come back from a long way off, but as he looked up he caught her eye, became very still. 'Go ahead, I'm listening.'

I want to have a baby. Your baby. It sounded so emotional, almost desperate put like that. Not a good start. But that heartfelt 'You've been away too long . . .' gave her the courage to press on.

'I wondered what you thought about starting a family,' she said.

He looked up, momentarily shaken, his eyes dark with something that might almost have been pain. Then he shook his head. 'Leave it, Abbie. This is not a good moment.'

Whatever reaction she had expected, it certainly wasn't that. 'Not a good moment'? What on earth did that mean? 'You did say we were apart too much . . . ' she began, trying to lift an atmosphere that had suddenly become about as light as a lead-filled balloon.

'And a baby would fix that?' Grey sat back in his chair, abandoning any further attempt to eat. 'That's a somewhat drastic solution, isn't it?'

Drastic? The second she had opened her mouth Abbie had realised the moment was all wrong, but it shouldn't ever be *that* wrong, surely? Confused, hurt, she said, 'I . . . I thought we both wanted children.'

'Eventually,' he agreed coolly. 'But we had an agreement, Abbie. No children until you're ready to give them your full-time care.'

'Yes, but — '

'Do you really think you can have it all?' he demanded, cutting off her protest, and she saw to her astonishment that he was now genuinely angry with her. 'Most of your friends manage it, I know, by cobbling their lives together with nannies and living from one crisis to the next. But they don't disappear into the wide blue yonder for a couple of weeks whenever a tantalising commission is dangled in front of them.'

'Neither do I! I never go anywhere without discussing it with you first.'

'But you still go,' he declared. 'That was the deal we made. God knows I miss you when you're away, Abbie, I've never made any secret of that fact — but it's a choice we both made right at the beginning. You said you'd need five years to establish yourself in your career, then you could take a break.'

'I don't remember carving it on a tablet of stone!' Suddenly the discussion was getting too heated, too emotional, but she couldn't stop. 'I . . . I want to have a child now, Grey.'

'Why?'

Because I love you and having your baby would be the most wonderful thing that could happen to me. His detached expression did not invite such a declaration.

In the absence of an immediate answer, he provided one for her. 'Because all your friends are having babies,' he said dismissively.

'Rubbish!'

'Cogently argued,' he replied.

'God, I hate it when you go all *lawyerish* on me,' she declared fervently. 'What would you do if I simply stopped taking the pill?' The words were out. It was too late to call them back.

But his expression betrayed nothing. 'Is that emotional blackmail, Abbie,' he asked, very quietly, 'or a statement of intent?'

Her face darkened in a flush of shame. She had always considered their marriage an equal partnership. Right now it didn't feel that equal, but a child needed two loving parents and it was a decision they had to make together. Slowly, deliberately she shook her head. 'I've been thinking about this for months, Grey,' she told him.

The planes of his face hardened

imperceptibly. 'And now you've made up your mind, you've decided to inform me of your unilateral decision?'

'It wasn't like that, Grey. I . . . I just wanted to be sure.'

'Well, I want to be sure, too,' he declared. Then, as if trying to claw away from the edge of some yawning precipice, he went on, more gently, 'What about your career? You're beginning to make a real name for yourself — '

'I don't intend to stop working, Grey,' she said, interrupting. Lord, if that was his only concern then there was no problem. 'I thought if we had a nanny I could get on with — '

The tight constraint finally snapped. 'Damn it, Abbie, a baby is not an accessory that every professional woman needs to prove that she's some kind of superwoman. I won't have a child of mine dumped at six weeks with a nanny while her mother gets on with her real life.' He flung his napkin on the table, pushed back his chair and rose to his feet.

'You don't understand!' she flung at

him. 'Why won't you listen to me?'

'I've listened. Now it's my turn to think. Months you said you'd been thinking about this? How many months? I think I should at least be granted as long as you.'

'Don't walk away from this, Grey,' she warned him. 'I'm serious.'

'So am I.' For a moment they stared at one another across the table as if they were strangers. Then Grey gave an awkward little shrug. 'We'll talk about it again in six months. Now, since I'm really not very hungry, I'll go and deal with the messages that have piled up on the machine.'

Abbie, stunned into silence, remained where she was. She didn't understand what had happened. One moment they had been sitting quietly having their supper and the next they were tearing emotional lumps off one another.

'Well, you really made a mess of that, Abigail Lockwood,' she told herself aloud. More of a mess than she would have thought possible. If she hadn't known better, she would have thought he didn't want her to have his child . . . But that was ridiculous. Grey loved to be around children. She had been the one who'd wanted to wait a while to give her career a chance. She almost wished she hadn't been so successful . . .

With a sigh, she gathered the plates, cleared away and collected her bag from the hall. If he had decided to work, then so would she; while he dealt with his calls she could download her laptop onto the PC. But before that she would insist that he listen to her. He might still oppose the idea of starting a family, but at least he would know she had no intention of dumping her longed-for baby with a nanny and departing for all corners of the globe at a moment's notice. Hardly any wonder he was angry if he thought that was her intention.

Grey, on the telephone, stopped speaking and looked up as she entered the study, placing his hand over the receiver. 'Give me a minute will you,

Abbie?' he asked. 'This is — ' She didn't wait to find out what it was, but backed out, closing the door behind her with a sharp snap.

'Abbie?' He found her a few minutes later, loading the washing machine.

'Where's your bag, Grey? You must have some washing if you've been away.'

'In the bedroom. Abbie, about the phone call . . . '

She didn't want to listen to him explaining why suddenly he had secrets where there had never been secrets before. She knew some of his work was highly confidential, but they had always shared a study; he trusted her discretion . . . Or maybe it wasn't work at all. The thought leapt unbidden into her head. She straightened, pushed past him and crossed the hall to the bedroom, where she unzipped his bag and began to remove his clothes.

Then she collected the clothes they had so carelessly jettisoned while under the shower. Two pairs of wet jeans? She glanced at the pair she was already

26

holding which had come from his bag. What kind of lawyer took jeans to a case conference, for heaven's sake? Not Grey. He had a wardrobe full of sober, well-cut suits that he kept for the office. And as she scooped up the pair he had been wearing she caught the faintest scent of woodsmoke that clung to the cloth, reminding her of the cottage.

He was still in the kitchen standing in front of the washing machine when she returned, so that she had to ask him to move before she could load the clothes.

'Excuse me, Grey,' she said stiffly.

For a moment she thought he wasn't going to move. Then he shrugged, shifted sideways. 'Abbie, will you stop fussing about and let me explain?' he demanded as she pushed in the clothes, keeping her eyes determinedly upon her task.

'Explain? You wanted to make a private telephone call. What's there to explain about that?' Everything, she thought as she banged the door shut, set the programme, and when she turned away he was standing in front of her, blocking the way.

'I know you're angry with me for not wanting you to have a baby right now — '

'Give the man a coconut,' she interrupted flippantly as she tried to sidestep him. But it wasn't true. She was angry with him for not wanting to talk about it, for not listening. It was so unlike him.

He caught her arm as she brushed past, held her at his side. 'I'm sorry if I seemed as if I didn't care. I do. And I will think about it . . . it's just that it's been a difficult couple of weeks.'

'Difficult?' She was immediately contrite. 'What's happened? Is it Robert?' she asked, remembering the earlier telephone call.

'Robert?' At her mention of his brother his eyes narrowed.

'You rang him earlier. I just wondered . . . ' She hesitated in the face of his guarded expression. 'I thought perhaps Susan had been causing more trouble.'

'No. It's not Susan . . . ' He gave another of those awkward little shrugs that were so out of character. 'I can't explain right now.'

'No?' She stiffened abruptly. 'Then I can't understand. If you'll excuse me, Grey?' she said with polite formality. 'It's been a very long day, and if I don't lie down right now, I think I might just fall down.'

He stared at her as if he couldn't believe what he was hearing. Well, that was fine with her. That made two of them who were having that kind of trouble today. He stepped back abruptly to let her pass, his jaw tight, a small angry muscle ticking away at the corner of his mouth. 'Then I certainly won't disturb you when I come to bed. Good-night, Abbie.'

She made it to the bedroom before the tears stung her eyes. What on earth was happening to them? They had been married for three years. Three blissfully happy years. Of course they'd had rows. Loud, throwing-the-china rows on more than one occasion, rows that had lasted for seconds, blowing away the tensions, before the most glorious and lengthy reconciliations. But never a row like this, that you couldn't put your finger on. A tight-lipped, hidden secrets, *polite* kind of row.

Something was wrong. She had sensed it from the moment of her arrival at the airport when he hadn't been there to meet her. He would normally have checked the answering machine from his hotel while he was away. He'd had plenty of time to get her message last night. But he hadn't. Something had happened while she was away. But what? She curbed the instinct to turn back and confront him. Demand to know. Things were bad enough.

True to his word, Grey didn't disturb her when he came to bed. Despite the long hours of travelling, sleep eluded her, but hours later, when Grey finally came to bed, she closed her eyes, and whether he believed it or not he didn't challenge her pretence. He didn't put on the light, but quietly slipped out of his clothes and lowered himself gently into the bed beside her, and after a moment he turned his back.

She opened her eyes in the darkness and lay for hours, listening to his soft breathing and thinking about the plans she had made so eagerly on her journey home. Was it possible, she wondered miserably, that she had left the decision not to accept any more overseas jobs just one assignment too late?

* * *

She woke to a room still darkened by the heavy velvet curtains drawn across the window, but the sunlight was spilling in from the hallway and she knew instantly that it was late. She lay for a moment in the silent flat, knowing that she was alone and hating it. She had hoped that the morning would bring some kind of reconciliation. Neither of them had behaved exactly brilliantly, but they had both been tired last night and she was prepared to acknowledge that, while Grey might have been a little more receptive, she might have picked a better moment to suggest a total upheaval to their lives.

Instead he had left while she was asleep. Gone to his office without even saying goodbye. She had intended to stay at home that day, attend to wifely things. Shop, prepare a good meal. Reclaim her surroundings from two weeks of Grey's bachelor housekeeping. Instead she found she had a need to reinforce herself as a person in her own right. And there was no better way of doing that than work.

She flung back the cover and slipped out of bed. But as she reached for her wrap she frowned. On the wall opposite the bed had hung a small Degas. Not a great painting — nothing that would set the galleries of the world at each other's throats — but very pretty and very genuine. It was gone. Had they been burgled while she was away and he hadn't wanted to frighten her? Was that why it had been a difficult week? Abbie flew to her jewellery box, locked in a small drawer in her dressing table, but it was there with all the pieces he had bought her during three happy years. She picked up the phone to call him at his office, then hesitated.

There was probably some perfectly logical explanation. Grey sometimes lent it to galleries for exhibition — maybe he had simply forgotten to mention it to her. They hadn't exactly spent the evening in close conversation. She replaced the receiver. That was probably it, she decided. It would wait until he came home.

Trembling just a little, she went into the kitchen to make some tea. On the centre island, where she couldn't possibly miss it, stood the silver bud-holder that Grey had bought her for their first wedding anniversary. In it was a red rose, a half-opened bud. And there was a note propped against the bud-holder — a plain sheet of paper, folded once. She opened it. 'I thought you needed to sleep. I'll see you this evening. Grey.'

That was all. No apology. But then he had taken the trouble to go out and find a rose for her before he drove into his City office. It wasn't quite like buying a pint of milk from the corner shop. It couldn't have been the easiest thing to find at seven-thirty in the morning. Yet why did she have the disturbing feeling that he might have found it a whole lot easier than waking her up and saying that he was sorry?

# 2

Two hours later Abbie, dressed in a loose-fitting pair of heavy slub silk trousers in her favourite bitter chocolate colour and a soft creamy peach top that glowed against her tanned skin and hair, bleached to a streaked blonde by the sun, was discussing the layout of her feature for the colour supplement of a major newspaper with her commissioning editor. Her photographs had been forwarded by courier and now the two of them were bent over the light box, deciding which ones to use.

'You've done a great job, Abbie. This photograph of the mother getting into that tiny plane to fly up into the hills to start looking all over again — '

'I tried to stop her. If only I could have gone with her . . . '

'No. That's the right place to end it. A touch of hope, bags of determination and courage. A mother alone, searching for her missing child. You deserve an award for this one.'

'I don't deserve anything, Steve,' she said, suddenly disgusted with herself for being so pleased with the finished result. 'I just hope she's all right. Anything could happen to her up there and no one would ever know.'

Steve Morley gave her a sharp look. 'You sound as if you've got just a little bit too emotionally involved in this one, Abbie. You were there to record what happened, not become responsible for the result. The woman has made her decision. It's her daughter. And your story will make a difference . . . '

'Will it? I wish I thought so.'

'Trust me,' he said firmly. 'Come on, I'll take you out to lunch.'

Trust. An emotive word. But without it there was nothing. Was too much time apart eroding that precious commodity between her and Grey? She would trust him with her life, and yet . . . and yet . . . There were too many gaps, too many empty spaces yawning dangerously between them. Baby or not, her mind was made up. She wouldn't be going away again.

As they made their way down in the lift Steve distracted her by asking her where she would like to eat, and reluctantly she let go of her thoughts about the future to concentrate on more immediate concerns. 'I've found this really good Indian restaurant,' he continued, 'but after two weeks on the sub-continent, I don't suppose you'd be interested — '

'You suppose right, Mr Morley,' she interrupted, very firmly. Then she grinned. 'Now, how good did you say that feature was?'

Steve groaned. 'L'Escargot?'

'L'Escargot,' she affirmed with a grin. 'Upstairs.'

Lunch was a light-hearted affair, with Steve bringing her up to date on what had been happening during her absence and offering several suggestions for future features.

'How do you feel about a month in the States for us?' He continued hurriedly as he saw she was about to object, 'Human interest stuff in the deep South — Atlanta. It's the sort of thing you're particularly good at. Although since your charming husband got a decent price for his Degas at auction last week I don't suppose you actually need the money,' he added, with an offhand little shrug.

The Degas? Sold? Despite the whirl of conflicting emotions storming through her brain she wasn't fooled by Steve Morley's casual manner. He had hoped to take her unawares, provoke some unguarded response. If he thought the Lockwood family were in any sort of financial trouble he would want to know. It was probably the whole reason for this lunch. 'You don't normally cover the art market, do you, Steve?' she asked, arching her fine brows in apparent surprise. 'I mean, doesn't that take brains . . . ?'

He grinned, aware that he had been

caught out, but was unrepentant. 'I cover everything that has the Lockwood name attached to it, and if you're ever seriously in need of funds, Abbie, I'm always deeply interested in brother Robert's doings.'

'I thought we had an agreement? You don't ask me about Robert and I'll continue to work for you.'

He shrugged. 'It doesn't hurt to remind you now and again that I'm always receptive to a change of heart.'

'Forget it. And Atlanta. I'm not in the market for overseas work for a while.'

'The old man getting a bit restive, is he?' He had gone straight to the heart of the matter, and she had known Steve too long to attempt to string him some line.

'Even the best marriage needs to be worked at, Steve.'

'I won't argue with that. I only wish my wife had been quite so dedicated.' He shrugged. 'And if the pretty piece I saw Grey having lunch with last week is anything to go by, I'd say you haven't left it a day too long.'

'Pretty piece?' Abbie felt the smile freeze on her face.

Steve shrugged. 'From what you said, I thought you must at least suspect something was up . . . '

'Suspect something?' It had been a moment's shock, that was all. On top of everything else that had happened she should have been reeling. But if there was one thing of which she was absolutely certain it was this: if her husband had been lunching with another woman, there had to be some perfectly rational explanation. 'Oh, Steve, really!' she chided, even managing a small laugh to show him how ridiculous such an idea was. But she knew it would need more than that. Taking his hand between her fingers, she regarded him solemnly with large grey eyes. 'Would you like me to tell you something that has just occurred to me?' she asked. 'Something rather amusing?'

Relieved that she was apparently not

about to have hysterics, Steve smiled. 'Fire away.'

'It's just that . . . well, I wondered what Grey would say if someone mentioned to him that they had seen me having lunch upstairs at L'Escargot with one of the best-looking men in London.' And she leaned forward and kissed him, very lightly on the lips, before releasing his hand. It was a reproach. A gentle one, but it wasn't lost on her companion.

'Ah,' he said. 'Point taken. I suppose I jumped to the most obvious conclusion because you were away . . . A bad habit. My only excuse is that I started out on a gossip column.'

'It's a bad habit that will cost you the biggest bowl of strawberries in this house,' she replied sweetly.

'Yes, ma'am,' he said, summoning the waiter, but somehow they didn't taste of anything very much, although she forced herself to eat every one. And when Steve dropped her off outside her home, she didn't go straight inside, but walked across the road to a small park, occupied in the middle of the afternoon by nannies, identifiable only by their youth and the expensive coach-built prams they wheeled before them in the sunshine, and middle-aged ladies walking small, immaculately groomed dogs.

Surely she was right? Grey was straight down the line. If he had found someone else he would tell her. He could never have made love to her like he had yesterday if he was having an affair, could he? Except that he had never before made love to her in that desperate, almost angry way. And then, afterwards, he had left her without a backward glance.

Oh, that was ridiculous, she chided herself. She was feeling bruised by their row, that was all. But even as she sat in the sunshine, convincing herself of the fact that he loved her, she wondered why she felt the need to do so. They were the perfect couple, after all. Teased by their friends because they were always the first to leave a party, envied for the freedom they were able to give one another, the almost transparent trust.

And yet were things quite so perfect? Grey's willingness to co-operate with a career that took her away regularly had always, to her, seemed a demonstration of how much he loved and trusted her. She had always rather pitied friends who hinted they would never leave a man that good-looking on his own for more than five minutes, let alone five days. But now little things that hadn't seemed important suddenly took on a new significance. Grey had had a series of late nights working on a difficult case just before she went to Karachi. Yet he had once said that the need to work late betrayed one of two things: a man incompetent at his job, or a man unwilling to go home to his wife. And Grey was certainly not incompetent.

She caught herself, unable to believe the direction in which her mind was travelling. The fact that Steve had seen him having lunch with another woman meant nothing. She was probably a client, or a colleague. Even if she was nothing whatsoever to do with his work she *trusted* him, for heaven's sake. It was certainly no more sinister than her lunch with Steve. The whole thing was utter nonsense. She was just edgy with him because of that stupid row. And if he had sold the Degas because of financial worries, that would certainly explain his reluctance to start a family, his reluctance for her to give up lucrative assignments. If only he had explained, trusted her. Trust. The word seemed to be everywhere today.

Happier, she was even willing to concede that his reaction to her immediate desire for a baby had been justified. She had been so full of her plans that she had expected him to leap into line without a thought. Well, she could start the necessary reorganisation of her life without making an issue of it. In fact she had already begun. No more overseas assignments.

She would tell him all about it when they were at the cottage. A couple of weeks at Ty Bach would give them a chance to talk when they were more relaxed, time to discuss the future properly. She should have waited until then to broach her plans. And, feeling considerably happier, Abbie stood up, dusted herself off and walked briskly back to the flat.

Yet Grey's key in the lock just after six brought an unexpected nervous catch to her throat.

'Abbie?' He came to the kitchen doorway and leaned against the door, smiling a little as if pleased to see her there. 'Hello.'

'Hello.' A little shy, just a little formal. 'You're early.'

'Mmm,' he agreed. 'I asked the boss if I could leave early so that I could take my wife out.'

'Idiot,' she murmured, laughing softly. 'You *are* the boss.'

'Obviously a very good one . . . ' he said, walking across to her and resting his hands lightly about her waist. There was only the slightest tenseness about

45

his eyes to betray what they both knew. That this was a peace overture. 'I said yes.'

So that was the way he was going to deal with it. Pretend last night had never happened. Love means never having to say that you're sorry? Maybe. She lifted her hands to his shoulders, raised herself a little on her toes and kissed him, very lightly. 'Thank you for the rose.'

'I'm glad you liked it.' His face relaxed into a smile. 'I risked life and limb climbing over the park railings to pick it for you.'

'Grey!' she gasped, her hand flying to her mouth at the idea of a sober-suited solicitor clambering over the park fence at dawn. 'You didn't!' He lifted one brow. 'Idiot!' she exclaimed. 'Suppose someone had seen you?'

'If it made you happy it was worth the risk.' He put one arm about her to draw her closer, and with his other hand he raked back the thick fringe of hair that grew over her brow and dropped a kiss there. 'Besides, I know I could rely on you to bake me a sponge with a file in it and ingeniously smuggle it into jail. Your cakes are so heavy that no one would suspect a thing.'

'Idiot!' she repeated, but this time flinging a punch at his shoulder.

'Possibly,' he agreed. 'And I've got something else.' He produced a pair of theatre tickets from his inside pocket and held them before her eyes. 'You did want to see this?'

'Grey! How on earth did you manage to get hold of them?' she demanded, eagerly reaching for them so that she could see for herself. 'They're like gold dust.'

He smiled at her reaction. 'You'll have to retract the 'idiot' first,' he warned her, holding them tantalisingly out of her reach.

'Unreservedly. Heavens, all this attention will go to my head,' she said happily, leaning her head against his chest.

'Oh? And who else has been spoiling you?'

'Only Steve Morley. He took me out to lunch,' she added, lifting her head to look into his eyes. Was she hoping for some immediate confession about his own lunch date? If so, she was disappointed.

'Lucky Steve,' he said, with just a touch of acid in his voice. It was not lost on Abbie. Grey had never said anything, but Abbie sensed a certain reserve in his enthusiasm for that particular journalist and his newspaper. But then, since they took particular relish in hounding his brother, Robert Lockwood, a politician and the most glamorous member of the government front benches — including the women — that was hardly surprising.

'Did he take you somewhere nice?' She told him and his brows rose to a satisfactory height. 'Spoilt indeed,' he said, releasing her and crossing to the fridge to extract a carton of juice. 'He must have been very pleased with your feature.'

'Very — in fact he immediately

offered me a month in America.'

'I'm impressed,' he said, without much enthusiasm, as he tipped the juice into the glass.

'And so you should be,' she declared, and, just a little peeved by the lack of congratulations, didn't bother to tell him that she had turned it down. 'You're apparently married to one hot property. Steve was talking about awards for the tug-of-love story.'

'Just as well I didn't leap at the chance of fatherhood, then.' He sipped the juice. 'So when will you be going?'

'You wouldn't mind?' she asked, heart sinking just a little. 'I've never been away that long before.'

'We made a deal, Abbie. I'm not going to start coming the heavy husband now you're on the brink of something special. You have to be available if you're going to be a star.'

Being a star was becoming less attractive by the day. 'I thought being good meant that you were able to pick and choose your assignments,' she said.

'Besides, what about our holiday? I'm looking forward to having you to myself for a couple of weeks.'

'You'd trade two weeks at an isolated cottage in Wales for a month in the States?' She would trade anything for two weeks alone with him, and it didn't matter where, but he didn't wait for her answer. 'Anyway, there's been a bit of a hitch about the cottage.'

'Oh? I thought it was all arranged.' Before she had gone away he had been full of plans. Most of them involving lying on the beach and doing absolutely nothing except making love for two weeks. He must have seen her disappointment, because he put down the glass and crossed to her.

'I'm sorry, but Robert wants to use the cottage this summer, Abbie. It's the one place the Press don't know about; even if they found out, it's hardly the easiest place to find, and the locals have a way of forgetting how to speak English when anybody starts getting nosy. He needs to spend some time

50

with his family.'

Abbie felt a little stab of guilt. She had a very soft spot for her brother-in-law. Grey's older brother was good-looking, brilliant — the youngest minister in the government. He should have been the happiest man alive. But he had a wife who kept him glued to her side with the threat of a scandal that would wipe out his career should he take one step to end their disastrous marriage. So he continued to play happy families for the benefit of the media, although he spent as much time as possible at his London flat and Jonathan, their son, was now at boarding school.

'How is Robert? I saw his photograph in the newspaper when I was on the plane. I thought he looked more at ease than I've seen him for a long time. Has there been some kind of reconciliation?' she asked. 'Is Susan going to the cottage with them?'

Grey didn't answer, although his mouth hardened into a straight line. 'Come on, let's go out and enjoy ourselves.' And it was only later, as she drifted off into sleep, that she remembered about the painting.

*　*　*

It was three days later that Abbie saw Grey with his 'pretty piece'. She had been shopping and had decided to drop in and see if he could join her for lunch in a local wine bar they occasionally went to.

Her cab had just dropped her off outside the office when she saw his tall figure heading purposefully along the road and then turning into the small park in the square around the corner from his office. She set off after him. If he'd bought sandwiches to eat in the park she would happily share them.

The good weather had brought out the office workers in droves, and they were sitting on benches and lying on the grass, soaking up the sun. Abbie lifted her hand to shade her eyes and swept the area for Grey. For a moment she didn't see him. Then she did. And in that moment she wished, more than anything in the world, that she hadn't seen him. That she hadn't followed him. That she had decided to stay at home and do some dusting. That she was anywhere but this small green City oasis.

A 'pretty piece' Steve had called her. Steve was right. But then he had a well-tuned eye when it came to a woman. She was small, with a delicate bone structure and the translucent complexion that so often went with very dark hair — hair that hung down her back, straight and shiny as a blackbird's wing. Abbie felt a sharp stab of jealousy as she recognised that special kind of fragility that made men feel protective — the kind of fragility that she had never possessed as a self-consciously gawky teenager, a tall young woman.

Grey was the only man she had ever known who had to bend to kiss her, but never in the way he bent now to tenderly kiss the cheek of his dark beauty. Then he put his arm about her shoulder as he leaned forward over the padded baby buggy she was wheeling, reaching out to touch the tiny starfish fingers of the infant lying there. It was a scene of such touching domesticity that if he had been some unknown man she would have glanced at the pair of them and thought what a perfectly charming picture they made.

Abbie shrank back into the darker shade of the trees, her heart beating painfully, her throat aching with the urgent desire to scream, her hand clamped over her mouth to make sure she didn't. She wanted to leave. Walk away. Run away from that place. The idea of spying on her own husband was so alien, so disgusting that she felt sick. But she remained rooted to the spot, unable to make her feet move, to tear her eyes from the two figures, or the baby lying gazing up at its mother, as they walked almost within touching distance of her on their slow circumnavigation of the path that rimmed the little park.

'If there's anything else you need, Emma, just ring me,' Grey said as they passed, blithely unaware of Abbie standing motionless in the shadow of the trees. The girl murmured something that Abbie couldn't hear and he shook his head. 'At the office unless it's an emergency.' Then the girl looked up at Grey, her dark eyes anxious. 'Yes, she came back a couple of days ago.' There was apparently no need for further explanation. 'I'll take you down to the cottage as soon as . . . '

As they moved on, turned the corner, his voice no longer reached her. The cottage. He had arranged to take this girl called Emma to Ty Bach. All that talk about Robert had been lies . . . lies . . .

No wonder he had wanted her to go to America. He had other plans for his summer vacation. And it was hardly surprising that he didn't want her to have a child. He hadn't wasted much time in arranging for a job-share wife, it seemed. But obviously one family at a time was enough.

No, Abbie. A small voice inside her head issued an urgent warning. You're leaping to conclusions. There might be a rational explanation. Must be. This was some girl from the office who had become pregnant, needed help. Or someone from the law centre. A client. No, not a client. He had kissed her, and kissing clients — even on the cheek — was asking for trouble. But something. Please God, something — anything. Think! But her brain was as responsive as cotton wool.

When the pair reached an unoccupied bench on the far side of the park, Emma sat down and Grey joined her, his arm stretched protectively along the back of the seat. They chatted easily for a while, laughed at some shared joke. Then Grey, glancing at his watch, produced an envelope from inside his jacket pocket. Emma took it, stowed it carefully in her bag without opening it and then, when Grey stood up, got quickly to her feet and hugged him. He held her for a moment, then, disengaging himself, he looked once more at the sleeping child and touched the baby's dark curls before turning to walk briskly back towards the gate.

There had been nothing in their behaviour to excite interest. No passionate kiss, no lingering glances. They had looked for all the world like any happily married couple with a new baby, meeting in the park at lunchtime.

Abbie instinctively took a step further back into the cover of the bushes as Grey approached the gate, but he looked neither left nor right. Then he crossed the road and stopped at a flower stall to buy a bunch of creamy pink roses, laughing at something the flower-seller said as he paid for them. A moment later he had disappeared from sight, and Abbie finally stepped out into the dazzling sunlight.

For once in her life — her ordered, planned, tidy life — Abbie didn't know what to do. And then quite suddenly she did. It was perfectly clear. She was a journalist. Not the foot-in-the-door investigative kind, but nevertheless a trained observer, with a mind cued to extract information as painlessly as possible from even the most reluctant of interviewees. If this were a story she would go across to where the girl was still sitting on the shady bench and find some way to strike up a conversation.

It shouldn't be difficult, for heaven's sake. Babies and dogs were a gift — guaranteed to make the most reserved people open up. She didn't want to do it, but she had to. And on legs that felt as if they were made of watery jelly, Abbie forced herself to walk towards the girl her husband had put his arm around and called Emma.

She had nothing in her mind. No plan. No idea of what she was going to say. But it wasn't necessary. As she approached the bench the girl looked up and smiled. No, not a girl. Close up, Abbie realised that she must be nearer thirty than twenty. A woman.

'It's really too hot for shopping, isn't

it?' she said as she saw Abbie's bags. Her voice was silvery, light and delicate, like the rest of her.

'Yes, I suppose it is.' Was it hot? She felt so terribly cold inside that she couldn't have said. But it was an opening and she sat down.

'Did you buy anything nice?'

A simple question. Difficult to answer, but she managed it. 'A shirt and a sweater. For my husband,' she added, unable to help herself. *No!* Put the woman at her ease — talk to her, her subconscious prodded her. Forget that this is personal. Treat it like any other story. 'And socks,' she continued. 'Men never seem to have enough socks, do they?' Smile. Make yourself smile. 'I have this theory that there is a conspiracy between the washing machine manufacturers and the sock-makers . . . '

Apparently the grimace that locked her jaw had been somehow convincing, because Emma laughed. 'You could be right. But I wouldn't care if I could only just go out and buy a pair of socks for my man. Unfortunately he has the kind of wife who would notice.'

'Oh?' Would she? Would she query strange socks in the laundry? Yes, she rather thought she would.

'I can't even keep things for him at my place. It would be so easy to get them muddled up.'

'I suppose so.' Abbie felt herself blushing at such unexpected frankness, yet she was well aware of how easily some people would talk about even their most intimate lives to perfect strangers. Especially if there were constraints on talking to family or friends. But the last thing on earth she wanted to discuss with this woman was her 'man's' wife.

She stated at the buggy. 'A baby is rather more personal than a pair of socks,' she said, forcing the words from her unwilling lips. But she had to be sure. 'The greatest gift of all.'

The woman's smile was full of secrets as she leaned forward and touched the child's fingers. 'That's what he said.

And, while he may leave me one day, I'll always have his child.'

'How old is he?' Abbie asked hoarsely, as jealousy, like bile burning in her throat, swept over her.

'Twelve weeks.' The woman called Emma brushed back the mop of dark hair that decorated his tiny head. 'He was born just after Easter.'

When Abbie had been steeping herself in the miseries of an African refugee camp. Had Grey been with this woman, holding her hand, encouraging her as she went through the pangs of giving birth to his son? No! Her heart rebelled. Surely it was impossible. And yet . . . She leaned over the buggy, letting her hair swing forward to cover her expression, and as she came face to face with the sleepy child she felt the blood drain from her face.

'He's beautiful,' she said, her voice coming from somewhere miles distant. As beautiful as his father had been as a baby.

Abbie remembered her laughter as

they had looked through a pile of old family photograph albums that they had found when they had cleared his father's house last year. Grey had been a bonny, bright-eyed baby, with a mop of black curly hair. The child lying in front of her might have been his twin.

'What's his name?' she asked, wondering that she could sit there and pretend that nothing was happening. Grateful for the numbness that somehow stopped her screaming with pain . . .

'Matthew.'

'Matthew?' Not Grey. At least he hadn't done that to her. But it was bad enough as with every painful scrap of hard-won fact she became more certain of just what he had done.

Matthew Lockwood. Founder of Lockwood, Gates and Meadows, solicitors. Grey's father, her dear, kind father-in-law, who had been dead for just a year. The child had been named for him.

'It's a lovely name,' she said quickly,

as she saw that some response was expected. 'Your . . . ' What? What could she call him? Friend? Lover? Her mouth refused to frame the word. 'He must be very happy.'

The woman leaned forward and touched the child, and his little hand tightened trustingly about her finger. 'Yes. He's thrilled with the baby — sees him whenever he can. But it's difficult for him.' She gave an awkward little shrug. 'His wife would never give him a divorce.'

And that finally broke through the pain and at last made her angry. 'Wouldn't she?' Abbie asked, a little grimly.

Now she knew, was absolutely certain, that Grey had been having an affair, deceiving her for at least the better part of a year. And in a way he was deceiving this woman too, with his lies. What had he said about her? How had he described her? Did the mother of his child know that when he left her bed, when he came home, he made sweet love to her as if . . . as if she was the only woman in the world?

Except that she wasn't. How could he do that? The man she loved, had thought she knew, was suddenly a stranger. A stranger who could, it seemed, smile as if his heart was all hers, tell her that he loved her, with the taste of this woman's kisses still upon his lips. The very thought was like a knife driving through her heart. How could she not have suspected? Not have seen the deceit in his eyes?

Only anger made her strong enough to sit there and carry on as if her world wasn't disintegrating about her, kept her head high as she turned to Emma, determined to discover just how far his lies extended. 'Has he asked his wife for a divorce?'

The woman gave the tiniest little shrug, the bravest of smiles. 'I wouldn't let him. A messy divorce would cause problems. With his job.' She gave a little shake of the baby's hand, turning her head away to hide the sparkle of tears.

'And we can't let Daddy have that, can we, sweetheart?' And the baby gave a broad, gummy smile.

It was a nightmare. A waking nightmare from which there could never be the escape of knowing that, no matter how dreadful, it had all been nothing but a horrible dream. But still Abbie pushed herself. The greater the betrayal, the more it hurt her, the better. With every thrust of the knife the easier it would be to do what she had once thought impossible and hate him.

'A divorce is no big deal these days, surely?' she insisted, denying herself any avenue of escape. Then she added hopefully, 'Unless he's your doctor?'

'Oh, no!' Emma exclaimed, horrified. 'He's ... ' She hesitated, as if she shouldn't say what he was. 'He's a lawyer.'

'I see.' And she did see — all too clearly. She had wanted to be sure and now Emma's words rang like the clang of doom, slamming the door closed on any possibility of doubt. His confession written in blood couldn't have been more convincing.

One of Grey's associates had been obliged to resign from the firm a year or so back, after having an affair with one of his clients. Her husband had turned nasty. She looked at the hand linked with the baby's fingers and she could see the telltale mark where a wedding ring had once rested. Was that how she had met Grey? Sobbing out her heartbreak in her husband's office? How impossible to refuse this fragile creature a comfortable shoulder to cry on. How easy to become emotionally entangled when your wife was away for weeks at a time.

'I don't mind, really. I knew all along that he would never leave her and I accepted that. At least I have Matthew.'

'Maybe it will all work out,' Abbie said dully. 'You mustn't give up hope. Things change.'

'Do you think so? I do sometimes dream about it.' Emma gave a little smile. 'Sometimes we can be together for a while and pretend. He has a cottage in the country that he shares with his brother. They're very close, and he's been so good about us using it . . . ' She glanced at her watch and leapt to her feet. 'Is that the time? I must be off — it'll soon be time for Matthew's feed.' She kicked off the buggy's brake, then paused to look down at Abbie, her face creased in concern. 'Are you all right? You look rather pale. Would you like a drink? I've got a can . . . '

'No!' She made an effort to pull herself together. 'Really, I'm fine. Thank you.'

Civilised behaviour. She should be scratching the woman's eyes out . . . but what good would that do? The woman called Emma smiled uncertainly. 'If you're sure?'

'Don't keep Matthew waiting for his lunch,' she said, forcing a smile. For a moment she remained where she was, watching Emma wheel the jaunty little buggy around the bright flowerbeds.

Then she too stood up and walked away, leaving her shopping behind her on the bench.

* * *

It was just after three when she arrived at the flat. Plenty of time to put the matter beyond all doubt before Grey came home. Not that there was any doubt left in her mind, but the evidence so far was purely circumstantial. She knew enough of the law to know the dangers of convicting on that.

She took the ring binders from the shelf and flicked back through the credit card accounts, meticulously filed month by month and paid on the dot. April. The day after she had flown out to Africa. Petrol purchased at a service station just inside the Welsh border. The same date. A trip to a supermarket in Carmarthen. She and Grey had shopped there the last time they had stayed at the cottage.

May. Where had she been in May?

Two days on an oil rig in the North Sea. More petrol. Another trip to the supermarket. She wondered what had headed the shopping list. Disposable nappies?

June. Another trip to Wales. Each entry was a knife wound in her heart.

The July account had not yet arrived, but the slips were there to prove his lie. On the day he had told her he was working in Manchester he had filled his petrol tank on the M4 near Cardiff. She remembered that he had been wearing jeans the day she'd come home, the scent of woodsmoke clinging to them. For a moment misery threatened to engulf her as she clung to the desk. Then, taking a deep breath, she forced herself to go on. There was no time for misery. Yet.

She put the file back on the shelf and took down the one containing the statements for Grey's personal account.

He hadn't even bothered to disguise his transactions. Large single payments of exactly the same amount for the last three months. And, remembering the envelope she had seen him pass to Emma, she had presumably witnessed another of those payments today. Tucked into the correspondence pocket of the file was a letter dated two days earlier from the bank, confirming that a trust fund had been set up in the name of Matthew Harper, using the proceeds of the sale of the Degas . . .

She had asked him what had happened to the painting. He had told her that it had been sold to help Robert out of a financial jam. And she had believed him.

# 3

For a long time Abbie sat there considering the possibility of revenge. Why not? She could wreck his career, drag in his brother, throw the kind of mud that, no matter how much you tried to wash it off, stuck like glue. One call to Steve and all the deceit, the lies would be plastered on the front page. Not because anyone would care about Grey or her, but because of Robert. And hurting Robert would hurt Grey. And she wanted to hurt him. She wanted him to know how it felt to be betrayed.

She knew all the right people to call in order to do the maximum amount of damage. She could break apart his life, make him suffer as she was suffering now. She was hunched over the desk, her head resting on tense little fists as she forced herself to believe what a week ago would have been unthinkable: that he had lied to her, deceived her, betrayed her. She had every right to hurt him with any weapon she could lay her hand on . . .

The shrill ring of the telephone sliced into her misery, startling her upright. She reached automatically for the receiver, then snatched back her hand, staring at it. Suppose it was Grey? How could she possibly speak to him? Behave in a civilised fashion when she felt positively savage?

The answering machine clicked in, and as she found herself listening to his warm voice inviting the caller to leave a message a tear splashed onto the bank statement. There was the long bleep of the tone.

'Grey? Are you listening to me?' Susan Lockwood's petulant voice whined into the machine. 'You'd better be listening!' She drew breath to spit her bile. 'You'd better tell your precious brother that he can't avoid me for ever. If he isn't home this weekend I'm talking to the newspapers. I'll tell them . . . '

Abbie put her hands over her ears, trying to shut out her sister-in-law's terrible threats. It was horrible, a nightmare, and five minutes ago she had been feeling exactly the same — wanting to lash out, hurt everybody because she was hurting. Eventually the stream of abuse stopped and she slumped over the desk, her head on her arms. Never, never, never, she promised herself, would she allow herself to become like that bitter woman, who was prepared to wreck her own life along with everyone else's in her possessive obsession with a man who could no longer stand even to be in the same room with her.

Abbie loved Grey. Being his wife had been the most perfect, the most beautiful thing in her life. He might have betrayed her, but the three years they had had together were full of precious memories. They were all she had left of him, and she would need those in the dark days ahead to keep her strong.

If it had been a straight fight between

the two of them things might have been different. She would have done everything, fought with every weapon at her disposal to keep the man she loved more than life itself. But the memory of a dark-haired woman, the very image of femininity, bent lovingly over her baby kept pushing itself to the forefront of her mind. It wasn't a straight fight. Break her heart as it might, that tiny baby needed his father far more than she needed a husband. And there was more than one way to love someone. Sometimes love meant letting go.

She picked up the telephone and dialled a number. 'Steve? This is Abbie. About that job in America — is it still open?'

* * *

Grey arrived home bearing the roses she had seen him buy. It had never occurred to her that he could be so cruel. But then it had never occurred to her that he could look her in the eye and lie to her. And he didn't know that she had seen him. That she had seen him touch his infant son and then cross the street and buy roses for his wife. It almost undid all her careful planning, all the effort that had gone into keeping back the tears.

'No!' she said quickly, drawing her hands back as he moved to hold her. If he touched her she would never be able to keep back the pain and her precious gift to him would be lost. 'Wet nail polish.'

'You can do it again,' he said, with that special little smile that she knew so well — an invitation to love that normally no amount of wet nail polish would ever have stopped her accepting.

'No time,' she said, twisting away to avoid him. She nodded in the direction of her bag standing in the hall and he followed her eyes. 'Steve called an hour ago. I'm booked on the evening flight to Houston. An oil well fire has broken out in Venezuela; I'm going with the team to cover it.'

A muscle tightened in his jaw and he dropped the flowers onto the hall table. 'That's rather short notice, isn't it?' He eyed the suitcase that was standing by her canvas bag. 'And rather more luggage than you normally take.'

She hadn't expected an argument, she'd thought he would be glad to see the back of her, but there wasn't time to think about that now. 'These guys aren't going to hang around while I catch up on my private life,' she said, turning to the mirror, smoothing a wayward strand of hair into place, lifting the collar of her crisp white shirt to a more flattering angle, giving herself time to get herself back in control. 'And the job fits in with the one I told you about. I'm going to stay on and do that afterwards.' He didn't say anything. 'So I'll need more clothes than I normally take . . . ' She rushed to fill the silence.

'You'll be away for six weeks . . . more . . . ' His face creased in a puzzled frown. 'I thought we were going away for a couple of weeks in August?'

'Away?' She discovered that she couldn't quite meet his eyes. 'You said the cottage wasn't available.'

'There's the rest of the world,' he said. 'Forget your oil men and I'll take you to the Maldives again ... ' She nearly jumped out of her skin as he put his hands on her shoulders and met her eyes in the mirror. 'You loved it there.'

The place hadn't mattered. She'd loved it because she had been with him. Because he had loved her. 'I c-can't,' she stammered.

'Can't?' He frowned. 'Or won't?'

She turned to face him. 'You're not going to come the heavy husband after all, are you, Grey?' she said, her throat so tight that she could barely get the words out. 'You were the one who said that if I wasn't available they'd never make me a star.'

His hands dropped to his sides. 'You didn't seem bothered at the time.'

'I was tired. Not thinking straight.' He didn't appear to be convinced. She would have to try a little harder. 'Oh, come on, Grey. Another year and I'll be able to pick and choose the jobs I want. I've worked hard to get where I am. It hasn't been easy and I'm not about to throw it away now.'

'I know that better than anyone, but I don't want you to leave like this — in a rush. You can catch up with your oil men later, Abbie. I think we need a little time together before you go. We need to talk.'

'*Later*, darling?' How *dared* he make it so difficult for her when she was trying to make it easy for him? 'Have you any idea what you're asking? If I'm not there to fly out with these guys . . . ' Her gesture to him through the mirror said it all. 'And there isn't time to brief anyone else. If I pull out, there'll be no feature at all.'

'Would that matter?'

'Matter?' She forced a laugh. 'What are you saying?' Her voice very nearly cracked in her attempt to make a joke of it.

Why wouldn't he just take the chance she was giving him? After the torments his brother had suffered she could understand his fear that she would cause trouble, why he would make every attempt to keep her happy — even make love to her as if he meant it. Susan's call had cleared her head, made her understand it all. Well, this way he would know that he was free, but he was making it so much harder than she had anticipated.

She could have taken the easy route. Been packed and long gone by the time he'd come home. How she had longed to do that. Just to disappear, never to have to see him again. Or she could have confronted him with the damning evidence, watched the love-light in his eyes die as he realised he no longer needed to keep up a front, a pretence that they still had a marriage. Even now, as the tension heightened between them, it would be so easy to tip it over into a fight and simply storm out. Except that he had never been a man to leave loose ends and he might just come after her.

'Of course it matters. I'd never get another job again, and what on earth would I do then?' she said, turning back to the mirror, flicking at her fringe — anything rather than face him.

'You could always stay at home. Last week you were desperate to have a baby.'

'You weren't very keen, as I recall.' She caught the touch of bitterness that had crept into her voice, forced a smile.

This was her last gift to him. A gift of love. Not wrapped in fancy paper, but in careless words calculated to wound, to destroy the fragile house of cards that their marriage had become. She was giving him the freedom to walk free without guilt. Guilt would not be a good start for a new life. And that was her only concern. The brand new life that he had created in a careless moment of passion — or of love, it hardly mattered. She had put her career before her marriage and was at least in some part to blame for what had happened, and she would take her share of the responsibility.

'You were right, of course. You always are. It was simply a case of my hormones going into overdrive.' She wouldn't be able to keep this up for much longer. She glanced at her watch, willing the taxi to arrive. 'I don't think I'm cut out for motherhood at all.'

'I don't believe you.' As she tried to pass him he caught her and held her, his face creased in a frown. 'What's going on, Abbie?'

'Going on?' She tried a careless laugh. It didn't work. 'Grey!' she protested as his fingers bit into her arm. 'You're hurting me!'

'There's something wrong. Tell me!'

'No!' she cried, then, 'No,' she repeated, more carefully. 'I'm just in a hurry. I'm afraid I haven't had time to — '

'Stop it! For heaven's sake look at yourself.' He swung her around so that they were both facing the mirror. Her cheeks were hectic, her eyes overbright from the desperate need to weep that she was keeping at bay by sheer will-power. 'Tell me, Abbie.' He gave her a little shake. 'You're not going anywhere until you tell me what's happening.'

'H-how are you going to stop me?' Her challenge sounded feeble enough to her own ears. Grey simply laughed. It wasn't a pleasant sound.

'You don't need to ask that, Abbie. You know how I'll stop you.' Her arm still grasped firmly in one hand, he raised his hand to her cheek and brushed it lightly with the back of his fingers. She shuddered. 'Catch a later plane, Abbie. It wouldn't be the first time, would it?' he murmured as, without haste, he began to unbutton her shirt. 'Remember?'

Remember? How could she ever forget? They had known one another ten glorious days when he had arrived at her flat just as she was getting ready to fly to Paris. She might even have made it if he hadn't decided to help her get ready . . .

'Grey, no,' she begged, desperate to stop him while she still had some control over her racketing senses. 'Please. The taxi will be here any minute.'

'It can wait,' he ground out harshly, his hand slipping beneath the flimsy lace of her bra, his long fingers cradling her breast, his thumb teasing its betraying, eager bud.

Her mind, sure of its purpose, screamed a silent protest. Her body refused to listen, cleaving to him as naturally as breathing while his insistent mouth demanded her utter slavery. She was helpless; she had always been helpless in his arms.

The long, insistent peal of the doorbell finally impinged on their consciousness, bringing them both back from some far place. But as they broke apart Grey raised his head to look at her from beneath heavy-lidded eyes. 'I don't want you to go, Abbie.'

And she could almost have believed him, except that when she opened her eyes she saw the faint smear of lipstick on the lapel of his suit and remembered that hours ago another head had rested there as he had briefly held the mother of his child in his arms.

That image brought her crashing back to sanity. 'If you have ever loved me, Grey, let me go. Please!'

'If I've ever . . . ' He looked as if she had struck him, releasing her so abruptly that she staggered back against the hall table. When she put out her hand to save herself it came down heavily on the abandoned roses, the sharp jab of a thorn spearing the pad of her thumb so that as her shaking fingers fumbled with the buttons of her shirt a tiny smear of blood stained the white cloth.

The bell rang again — an impatient tattoo. Grateful for the interruption, she turned from him and stumbled to the door, flinging it open. 'Will you take this bag?' she asked the driver. 'I'll bring the other one.' She picked up the canvas bag and turned unwillingly to face Grey. But he wasn't in the hall, and for a moment she thought she might scream out her agony for everyone to hear. Then suddenly he was there. Taking her hand in his, he fixed a small plaster to her bleeding thumb, and that . . . that was just so much worse.

He lifted her hand to his mouth, kissed the tip of her thumb. 'Take care of yourself, Abbie,' he said, all emotion clamped down under his masked expression. 'Ring me to let me know you've arrived safely.'

He bent towards her as if to kiss her, but she stepped back before he could touch her. And, because she was on the edge of breaking down, of letting out all the pain, all the heartbreak that she had been keeping under lock and key while she acted out the role of a careless wife, she turned and fled down the stairs without a word.

*  *  *

Abbie was hot. She had arrived in Atlanta expecting her senses to be assaulted by magnolia-scented air and the ante bellum mansions of the old South, only to find the skyscraper skyline of a modern city that might just as well have been New York — except that it was hotter.

She was wearing nothing but a silk wrapper, but even so her motel room seemed like a steam bath in the summer heat. She continued tapping her first impressions of the city into her laptop nevertheless, determined not to allow herself the luxury of a cold shower until the job was done.

A sharp rap at the door disturbed the flow of her writing and she paused, irritated at the interruption, to push her damp hair back from her forehead. But then everything was irritating her right now.

'Who is it?' she demanded.

'It's me,' a deep voice replied, and, startled, she crossed swiftly to the door and flung it open.

'Steve!' She stared at him in astonishment. 'What in heaven's name are you doing here?'

'The features editor collapsed trying to prove that he could still play five sets of tennis.' He grinned. 'Someone had to step in and take his place at the last moment . . .' His shrug was eloquent.

'So nobly, above and beyond the call of duty, you volunteered,' she said, somewhat cynically. 'And who's doing your job?'

'This is the silly season, Abbie. I was going on holiday anyway.'

'How convenient. And how nice of the paper to pick up the tab for you.'

'I'm here to work,' he protested. 'I thought you might be glad to see me. Aren't you going to invite me in?'

Conscious that she was wearing nothing beneath her silk wrapper, she shrugged a little awkwardly, but stepped back. 'Do you want a cold drink?' she asked.

'No, thanks, but I could do with a shower. My room isn't available for another hour and I'm about to melt.'

She glanced at her watch. 'You've got ten minutes,' she said, waving in the direction of the bathroom. 'Then you'll have to find someone else's time to waste. I've got an appointment.'

'Sure.' He didn't seem in the least put out by her less than enthusiastic welcome. 'I'll just get my bag from the car.'

A few minutes later, with the noise of the shower as a cooling backdrop, she was putting the finishing touches to her piece when there was another rap at the door. Abbie frowned, but this time refused to be diverted from her task, ignoring the sound as she typed in the last few sentences. The knock was repeated — louder, more insistent.

'Just a minute!'

But as she pressed the 'save' button she heard the door open behind her, and spun in her seat to find Grey already inside, the door closed, his tall figure barring the exit.

'Grey,' she said foolishly, rising to her feet. 'I — I didn't expect . . . H-how did you find me?'

'Were you hiding, Abbie? I was beginning to wonder.'

'I . . . um . . . ' Not hiding, exactly, but then she hadn't expected him to follow her. She had given him his freedom and she had expected him to take it and run. But he was here, in her motel room, regarding her intently from beneath heavy-lidded eyes. It was a look at once arousing and terrifying, and her breasts responded, peaking beneath the flimsy silk wrapper that clung seductively to her overheated body. Her cheeks suffused with fierce colour and she wanted to clutch the silk about her protectively, but that would only make things worse.

'You didn't phone me,' he said at last.

'The Venezuelan oil fields were a little short on facilities for personal calls — ' she began, but he wasn't interested in excuses.

'At first I thought you were just making me suffer a little because I'd tried to pressure you into staying with me. I mean, what other reason could there possibly be? And I knew that if something was wrong your paper would be in touch fast enough. Dear, kind Steve would phone me himself.'

Steve. She clamped down on her lips, tried not to look towards the bathroom. The shower had stopped running; it was quiet. Surely if he heard Grey's voice he would have the sense to stay put?

'But after a week, I thought you were overreacting just a bit, so I phoned the paper and asked dear, kind Steve's secretary for a contact number. You were on the move, she said, and could she pass on a message? I thought since our holiday had been cancelled we might spend a few days together sipping mint juleps under the southern stars. I wanted to check on the best time to come. She said she would ask you to ring me.'

Something like a moan escaped Abbie's lips and he paused, inviting her to speak. But she shook her head. He was angry. It was a chillingly restrained anger that froze her to the core, so that despite the heat she shivered.

'I *imagine* she passed on the message. But you didn't ring me, did you, Abbie? Instead of a phone call from my loving wife, I received this.' He took a letter from his jacket pocket and flung it on the table beside them. 'I would have thought, after three years of marriage, that I might at least rate some kind of explanation. Not just a letter from a stranger informing me that my wife has applied for a divorce on the grounds of irretrievable breakdown of marriage. Would you care to tell me when our marriage broke down, Abbie? I seemed to have missed it.'

She shook her head, unable to speak.

'Talk to me, Abbie!' The cool tone of his voice sharpened and she shrank back against her desk. 'Oh, for heaven's sake, I'm not going to . . . Just talk to me, Abbie. I'm not that unreasonable, am I? We've never run away from problems.' He took another step towards her, but as she drew back even further he stopped, raked his fingers through his hair.

'If this is about having a baby — ' He stopped as he saw that he had hit a nerve. 'So that's all it is.' Relief seemed to swamp him momentarily. 'I'm sorry, Abbie. Truly sorry. I reacted with about as much sensitivity as a concrete mixer, but if it's that important to you I'm sure we can work something out — '

'Work something . . . ?' She closed her eyes as words utterly failed her. He wanted her to come back? He was prepared to let her have a baby and carry on with his double life?

'The last few months have been difficult,' he continued. 'You've been away too much and I've had a lot on my mind . . . ' He was closer. As her eyes flew open his hand slipped about her waist and he touched her cheek with the tips of his fingers. 'Talk to me, Abbie,' he murmured softly, as she shivered helplessly against him. 'Don't shut me out.'

It was unbearable. She would never

have thought it was possible to miss anyone so much. They had been apart for longer, but then there had always been the promise that in a few days they would be together. Now, seeing him like this, his eyes lying to her, his gentle hands lying to her, it was almost more than she could bear.

She had thought that once she was away on the other side of the Atlantic, once she had instituted divorce proceedings, he would seize the chance to make a clean break and start a new life with Emma and Matthew. She had never anticipated that he would come after her and demand . . . explanations.

She stiffened, wrenched herself away from the drugging pleasure of his touch. 'I shouldn't have just left like that.' She held herself so rigid that she thought she might break. 'I'm sorry, Grey, but you're right. I've been away too much. When I came home last time nothing seemed to work for us. I suppose we've just grown apart. I thought it would be easier like this . . . '

'Easier?' For a moment he didn't seem to understand. 'To run away?'

His hands grasped her shoulders as if he wanted to shake some sense into her. But he restrained himself, biting down hard on his lip, so that the muscles in his jaw knotted with the effort. For a moment it was deathly quiet in the spacious motel room.

'Easier?' he repeated, more quietly, relaxing his grip so that he was no longer hurting her. But he didn't let go. 'I don't believe you, Abbie. You're not that kind of coward. And if you think it was easier for me, I have to tell you that you are mistaken.'

It had been so hard. Every day. Making herself get up, get on with the job, when all she'd wanted to do was turn her face to the wall and die. But it wasn't in her nature to lie down and let life walk all over her. He had accused her of wanting to have it all. Well, she had discovered the hard way that she couldn't. But every day she got up, put on her make-up and her prettiest clothes, and got on with the only life that was left to her. Work. And that would have to be her cover story now.

'I wanted a clean break, Grey,' she said, lifting her head, forcing a hard edge into her voice. 'I'm staying in America. You were right. I can't have a career — not this career — and a marriage. You need more than I can give you.'

'You've decided that, have you?' His eyes, those meltingly warm brown eyes, hardened as she had never seen them harden before. 'All by yourself? Perhaps I should remind you exactly what we've had for the last three years.'

In one swift movement he tugged at the tie of the flimsy silk gown and it slipped treacherously away from her body, leaving her defenceless against his raking glance. Then he reached for her, his hands enfolding her narrow waist and drawing her against him.

Certain now of easy victory, he tipped back her head and stared down into her face. 'What do you say, Abbie?'

95

Why was he doing this? Why had he come to torture her with his presence when she was trying to make it easy for him? 'Oh, come on, Grey,' she said, her voice as brittle as glass. 'We've had a lot of fun, but I've been spending more and more time away, not less. You need more than that. Deserve more than that . . .'

Her voice trailed away as she realised how close she was to betraying herself. That wasn't the way. She didn't want his guilt on her conscience; she wanted him to walk away and never look back. It was her final gift to him. A gift of love.

'I . . . I'm sorry, Grey. I simply don't love you any more.'

His eyes continued to regard her with a puzzled expression. 'You're lying, Abbie.' His hands on her arms might have tightened fractionally, but his voice remained cool, restrained; only the whiteness where his jaw muscles clamped down on his emotions betrayed how close to the edge he was.

'Lying?' From somewhere she conjured up a careless lift of her shoulders. 'What's the matter, Grey, can't your ego take it? I wanted to let you down lightly, but if you must know . . . the truth of the matter is . . . ' She faltered. The brazen lie did not come easily to her lips. 'The truth is that journalists are a clannish group. They always use the same hotels. It's like a club where you meet old friends, have a few drinks and — well . . . sometimes rather more than a few drinks . . . ' Her throat hurt so much she didn't know how the hateful words managed to creep out. 'Things happen . . . '

'Really? And then you run home and tell your husband that you want to have his baby?'

He didn't believe her. She'd told him that she had affairs in hotels with whoever happened to be around and he didn't believe her. He was angry enough to kill, but he didn't believe her. Her heart rejoiced at that, but her head knew that it wouldn't do. She had to make him believe her lies.

But she couldn't meet his eyes and lie, so she turned away as if in shame. 'I thought if I had a child, if I didn't have to go away again, it would be all right.' The silence was awful. She looked up then, and flinched at his face, masked with horror, but there was no turning back. 'But then, as soon as I was back in the office . . . '

Something died in his eyes. Some light. And as he took a sharp step back she knew she was close to achieving her aim. Close to making him hate her. It would be easy now. She moved after him, the air lifting the light robe away from her glistening skin, and she looped her arms about his neck, pressing her body against his. 'But sex with you was the best, Grey.' Her voice was little more than a husky murmur as she forced it through the pain. 'If you want to give it one last whirl for old times' sake . . . ' And she pressed her lips against his.

Even as she felt him stiffen, felt his

hands tighten to push her away, the click of the bathroom door was gunshot-loud in the silent room. Grey's head came up sharply at the sound.

As she swung round she saw Steve, fair hair slicked back from the shower, nothing but a towel wrapped about his waist, standing in the doorway.

Grey's eyes dropped to hers. 'I see. I appear to have been singularly stupid.' He pulled the edges of her gown together and tied it firmly about her waist before stepping clear of her. Then he turned to confront the man standing in the doorway. 'Abbie was trying desperately hard to protect you, bury you in a host of lovers — anything to get rid of me. If you had stayed put for another five seconds she would have succeeded — '

*No!* Abbie clutched at Grey's arm as his hands bunched into fists, but no sound came from her throat as he brushed her aside, crossing the room in a stride.

Steve did not move. 'Go on, hit me,'

he invited. 'I can see the headline now. MINISTER'S BROTHER IN MOTEL BRAWL — ' That was when Grey's fist crashed into his chin, sending him flying back into the bathroom.

For a moment he stood over the prone figure. 'Anything to oblige, Morley,' he said. 'Have a nice day.' Then he swung round and strode out through the door, without so much as a glance at Abbie.

For a moment she remained motionless, unable to do or say anything. When she had made the decision to let her husband go in the most painless way possible, to take to herself the pain of loss and the anguish of guilt as her parting gift to him, she could never, in all her wildest fantasies, have imagined that pure emotion could have such a physical pain, that her heart breaking in two would hurt just as surely as if she had broken a bone.

And as she stared at the open door through which Grey had walked away from her for ever it began to retreat, to grow smaller as the blood pounded louder and louder in her ears. She put out her hand as if to call it back, and it was her hand that hit the floor first.

★ ★ ★

When she opened her eyes she was staring at the ceiling, and for a moment nothing made sense. Then a cool flannel was placed on her forehead and she turned to see Steve, standing looking down at her.

'You fainted, Abbie. Just lie still for a moment.'

And then everything did make sense, and she groaned, trying to sit up even as Steve pushed her gently back onto the bed. 'Please don't put this in the paper.' There was no answer. 'Steve? For me?'

'Why not?' he demanded. Then added more reasonably, 'I would have thought that after what he's done to you it would give you the most thorough satisfaction to see him sued for assault.'

She groaned. 'Please! I . . . I couldn't bear it.'

'Most women in your position would give their eye-teeth to embarrass the man who had betrayed them. Embarrassing an entire government into the bargain would surely be the icing on the cake?' She shook her head. 'No? Why should *you* be so damned noble about it?'

'I . . . I don't expect you to understand.'

He gave a little shrug. 'Perhaps I understand more than you think.' He rubbed his chin, already darkening from its contact with Grey's fist, then sat on the edge of the bed. 'It must have been quite a shock to find me in your bathroom after he had flown all the way to Atlanta to be with you.' He regarded her thoughtfully, his forehead creased in a deep frown. 'It seems an odd thing to do, don't you think, when he has a surrogate wife lined up at home?'

Steve might not be able to work it out — he didn't have all the facts

— but she could make a good guess at the reason. Grey was covering himself. He would be able to stand up in court and tell the judge that he had done everything in his power to save his marriage. He had even flown across the Atlantic to plead with his wife to come back to him. Or maybe he really did want to carry on with things just the way they were . . . No. That hardly bore thinking about. In fact she refused to think about it for another second.

'I'd better do something about that bruise,' she said abruptly, swinging her feet to the floor and fetching some ice from the fridge. 'I'm just sorry you were involved in all this,' she went on, sitting beside him on the bed and applying a makeshift ice-pack to his face.

'Yes, well,' he said, wincing a little. 'Serves me right for helping myself to other people's bathrooms, I suppose.' He searched her eyes. 'Grey's knuckles will be just as sore as my chin, but I've got you to give me first aid. I think I know who I'd rather be at the moment.'

He put his arm about her shoulders. 'You know that, Abbie, don't you?'

There was a shocked moment when Abbie realised that Steve was offering considerably more than his broad shoulder to cry on. She could hardly blame him. He was an attractive man, and most women would probably be very happy to accept the easy comfort of his arms. But there had only ever been one man in her life, and she wasn't about to break the habit of a lifetime. She eased herself away from the casual embrace and stood up, putting a safe distance between them before she turned to face him.

'I'm sorry, Steve,' she said. 'But I believe it's time you booked into your own room.'

He rose to his feet and gave a little shrug. 'Of course. You said you had an appointment. If you don't feel up to it, perhaps I could take over?'

'No, thanks. I think you'd be better off lying down quietly in your room, with an ice-pack on that bruise.'

# 4

'Abbie? Have they come?' Polly burst through the door, dumping her school bag with a triumphant 'Yes!' as she saw the line of cardboard crates in the study. 'Can I help you unpack?'

Abbie regarded the boxed remnants of her marriage. 'I'd only have to pack it all again when I find a flat of my own,' she said unenthusiastically.

'But that could take months.' Polly, seventeen, had a directness that wasn't any easier to take just because she was so often right.

'Not if I can help it. I'm just . . . um . . . housesitting while your parents are away.' *Baby*sitting was the term Polly's mother had used, but that wouldn't go down too well. 'Your mother may be a dear friend, but she certainly won't want me as a permanent lodger.'

'Well, you'll need your computer,'

Polly pointed out. 'You said so.'

'Did I?' The truth was that Abbie had no desire to confront the possessions that Grey, so anxious to be rid of every reminder of her, had put into storage, sending an inventory to her solicitor. The sigh that escaped her was involuntary. It was six months since she had left him. Long enough, surely, for the jagged edges of heartache to have worn smooth?

It wasn't as if she had sat around and moped. She had been inundated with work after the appearance of the tug-of-love story, and on the run from one commission to the next she had been able to keep one step ahead of the pain. But all it had taken to sharpen the heartbreak into agonising focus had been a pile of ordinary cardboard boxes, and finally the urge to weep swept over her.

'Abbie?' Polly's voice had lost its eager certainty. 'Are you all right? I didn't mean to upset you . . . '

'Upset me?' She blinked back the

sting of tears and briskly picked up the contents list that had arrived with the boxes, meticulously written in Grey's clear, bold handwriting. Her books, files, clothes, the collection of fine china figures that had been gifts for birthdays, anniversaries, dull Mondays, happy Wednesdays — any excuse had done when Grey saw something that he thought she would like. Things she loved, things she dreaded facing. Each carefully listed. 'Of course not. And you're right. I do need the computer, and some more winter clothes.'

The decision made, it should have been easy. Her computer was a work tool. Hardly endowed with emotion. And yet when it had been new and terrifying she had constantly turned to Grey for help. He had grinned and leaned over her to press some magic key that made sense of everything. He had always known the magic keys to press. And as she hesitated now over the cables she heard his laughing voice in her head. 'Parallel printer . . . it goes there, see? It's easy.' She swallowed hard against the lump in her throat and pushed the connection home. Easy.

'Which box are your clothes in?' Polly asked, looking about her.

'That one,' she said, with a silent prayer of thanks to whichever kindly deity had prompted Grey to list everything, sparing her any unexpected confrontation with memories that would jar loose the fragile protective shell she had erected about herself.

But life was never that simple. As Polly scored through the thick tape and folded back the lid of the box Abbie saw the leather-bound album. A photograph album. Deliberate? Or had Emma found it and dumped it there without telling him? It hardly mattered. The shock was just as great.

'I love other people's photographs,' Polly said, idly flipping the pages. 'Wow! You look fabulous in a bikini, Abbie. Where is this?'

'The Maldives,' she said faintly. She didn't have to look. She knew the album. Honeymoon photographs. They had taken silly photographs of one another with silly expressions on their faces because they were so happy.

'Is this your husband?' Polly asked. Her voice seemed to be coming from a long way off. 'He looks just like Jon's father.'

'Jon?'

'A boy I know. At school. His dad's a politician — you must have seen him; he's always on the television . . . ' Her voice dried up as she looked across and saw the tears pouring down Abbie's cheeks. 'Oh, Lord.' She snapped the album shut. 'I'm sorry. I shouldn't have said anything. Can I get you a cup of tea? Or a drink? Brandy? Mum usually dishes that out for cases of shock . . . '

'It's all right, Polly.' She brushed the tears away with the palm of her hand. 'It just caught me by surprise, that's all.'

She crossed to the box, deliberately opened the album and turned the pages slowly. 'Did you say that your friend was called Jon?' she asked as the painful images flashed by. White-powdered beaches, hibiscus flowers, Grey snorkelling, his powerful body eerily green under water.

'Well, it's Jonathan actually,' Polly answered. 'Jonathan Lockwood. Oh, Lord!' She clapped her hand dramatically over her mouth. 'That was your married name!'

Robert's London flat was not far from Polly's home; it was hardly surprising that she and Jonathan would go to the same school. 'He's my husband's . . . Grey's nephew — '

'Grey? You mean *Grey* is your husband? But Jon talks about him all the time. There was an enormous row when he ran away from boarding school at the beginning of the Christmas term, and Grey told his father that it was time he sorted himself out and put his family before his work.'

'Did he? Well, he was right.' She had learned that too late. Abbie looked up. 'What about his mother?'

'She comes up to London some-times, I think . . . What's she like?'

'Susan?' A woman who took loyalty and love and used them as weapons. 'I never saw much of her,' she said, turning another page of the album. Grey smiled back at her.

Her hand hovered over the image, briefly touching the dark, straight brows that she so loved, the twist of his mouth as he smiled into the lens, the long, arrow-straight nose. Loving him was a feeling of such intensity that it hurt. Every night she promised herself that the next day would be easier. But every morning she woke up and was forced to face the truth once more. It didn't get easier. Each day was harder to bear. The image began to swim and then Polly was pushing a glass into her hand.

'Sit down. Drink that slowly.'

'I'm supposed to be looking after you, Polly,' she protested feebly as she sank onto a chair. Some babysitter.

'I don't need looking after. Mum thinks I'm a baby, but I'm not.'

'No.' She took a reluctant sip of the brandy. 'But with me here to keep an eye on things she can visit her new grandson without worrying about you.' She looked up at the pretty, bright-eyed girl and tried to remember what it was like to be on the brink of womanhood. Those intense, brittle feelings that one day made you feel on top of the world and the next in the depths of despair. A wonderful age, but a dangerous one too. Perhaps she should be taking her role a little more seriously. 'Are you and Jon . . . close friends?' she asked.

The girl flushed slightly. 'I won't bring him here if it would bother you.'

'It's all right, Polly. But I wouldn't want to embarrass him . . . Just warn me and I'll hide upstairs.'

'You still love him, don't you?' She made a gesture towards the album. 'Grey, I mean. Why did you split up?'

Her mother had never asked. Margaret had simply offered open arms and an open door. Seventeen was different. It was an age when you poked at life with a blunt stick, blissfully unaware that there were hornets' nests lying in wait for the unwary. But it was probably better to tell the girl the simple truth than have her inventing some fanciful drama.

'He had an affair, Polly,' she said, matter-of-factly. 'It happens every day.'

'An affair? But — '

'Come on,' Abbie said firmly, cutting off the question. 'I thought you were going to help me unpack these clothes.'

She seized the red cloak with determination, but as she shook out the creases she caught the faintest scent of dry leaves and bonfires and Grey, and without warning the memory of that first crazy Sunday together, when they had walked in St James's Park, rose up and overwhelmed her.

She had been to a party on the Saturday evening but had left early, pleading a headache. But she hadn't slept, haunted by the face of an unknown man who had glanced at her once, capturing her, holding her prisoner with his warm brown eyes for the space of a heartbeat, no more.

He hadn't looked at her again. Why would he have done? He had arrived with a delicate, exotic beauty who barely reached his shoulder, her eyes and hair as dark as night — the kind of woman who always made Abbie feel gawky and every last inch of her five feet ten inches. But her own eyes had strayed in his direction more than once, drawn irresistibly to the impressive black-clad figure who had so easily dominated the room. They had only dropped by on their way to somewhere grander, to leave a present and wish their hostess a happy birthday, and Abbie had felt a sense of something close to relief when they left. But this briefest of encounters had been oddly disturbing, and shortly afterwards she had made her own excuses and gone home.

After a sleepless night, the imperious ring on her doorbell just as the red autumn sun crept over the horizon had been hardly welcome. Crawling unwillingly from bed, Abbie had pushed the tousled mop of hair from her face, tugged on her dressing gown and pulled open the door, expecting to find a neighbour desperate for milk. But it hadn't been a neighbour. It had been him.

Shock had stilled the complaint poised on her tongue, and this time his eyes had remained on her face as without a word spoken between them he had stepped over the threshold and shut the door behind him.

'You really are that tall,' he said, as if he couldn't quite believe it.

If he'd woken her up to discuss her height . . . 'Five foot . . . ' Abbie considered taking off an inch. Changed her mind. He wasn't the kind of man you could fool. ' . . . ten.'

His mouth straightened as if he had read her mind. 'Only ten? Not ten and a half?' He was laughing at her, but she didn't mind. Perhaps she was floating. It felt as if she was floating, and that would make her look taller. Whatever the reason, she didn't contradict him. And she didn't move even when he reached out his hand and touched her cheek with the tips of his fingers.

'My name is Grey Lockwood. I'm a lawyer, thirty years old, and I've never been married. Until last night I'd never been in the least bit tempted.' He regarded her steadily. 'But I've spent the entire night thinking about kissing every single inch of you, Abigail Cartwright,' he said, with the utmost seriousness. 'All seventy of them. I couldn't wait any longer.'

She knew she should be indignant, outraged by this dawn raid on her emotions and heaven knew what else. But she wasn't. She didn't ask how he knew her name, or even how he had found her. Instead, equally earnest, she simply said, 'Me too.'

'That's all right, then.' His slow smile was oddly seductive, drawing her to him until his hands were gently cupping her face, his long fingers sliding through her sleep-tousled hair. 'I'll start, shall I? And we'll take it from there.' He seemed to look at her for ever, as if imprinting her upon his memory before he kissed her, slowly, thoughtfully, tenderly. And it was, she decided, a great deal more than all right.

She held the soft wool of the cloak against her cheek now, remembering. Her friends had predicted disaster as she had been spun headlong into a whirlwind of romance. It was too fast, they'd warned her. She wasn't experienced enough to handle a man like Grey. But, for once in her sensible, organised life, she hadn't listened to the voice of reason. It *had* been crazy. She knew that. Crazy and blissful and quite perfect.

Autumn walks in St James's Park with the scent of bonfires in the air followed by afternoon tea at the Ritz. A picnic on a deserted October beach. A stolen Wednesday afternoon at the Victoria and Albert Museum. And roses. He'd given her so many roses.

They had wanted it to last for ever and so, six breathless weeks later, they had been married.

With no family of her own, she'd had no desire for a huge church affair. Instead they'd had a beautifully intimate wedding, with just his father and brother and a few close friends to witness their vows to one another. It had all seemed like some glorious fairytale. For a long time it had seemed that they would make 'happy ever after'.

Abbie wondered what had happened to the exotic, dark-eyed beauty that Grey had been with that first time she saw him. She had been the daughter of some wealthy South American client, passing through London and needing an escort to the ballet. She sighed. Clearly that dark, delicate beauty had made a lasting impression on Grey.

'I think I should get this stuff cleaned before putting it away,' she said flatly to Polly as she dropped the cloak back into the box. That would deal with the treacherously lingering scents that sent her vulnerable memory winging back to happier days.

'I think you should finish your brandy,' Polly said, regarding her with daunting pity. 'It'll do you good.'

'Maybe.' Abbie regarded the half-filled tumbler doubtfully, and without warning her sense of humour bubbled through the painful memories. 'But do you feel capable of carrying me to bed?'

★  ★  ★

Abbie lay back on the sofa, put her feet up and groaned. 'I wouldn't have believed there were so many awful flats in the world.'

Polly looked up from her textbook. 'I expect, subconsciously, you're looking for somewhere like the lovely flat you shared with Grey,' she said earnestly.

'I'm doing nothing of the kind,' Abbie snapped, aching feet and a wasted day having severely blunted her patience. 'My subconscious is well aware that I couldn't possibly afford it.' Then she lifted her head and looked at the girl. 'How do you know it was lovely?'

Polly blushed fiercely. 'Jon took me there.'

'You persuaded Jon to take you to meet Grey?' Abbie was horrified. She had attempted to curb Polly's romantic hopes that her marriage might be mended, but any opportunity to talk about Grey had been sweet and it had seemed harmless enough . . .

But even as she sat up, determined once and for all to put a stop to the girl's foolish fantasies, something else occurred to her. What had Polly said to Grey? He believed she was swanning about the world without a thought in her head for anything but her career. If he were to discover that she was living quietly in London, looking after a seventeen-year-old while her mother was away in Australia acquainting herself with her new grandson, he might begin to wonder . . . And she didn't want him wondering. He was too sharp for that . . .

'It is *so* lovely,' Polly continued,

totally unaware of the alarm she had provoked in Abbie's breast. 'The bedroom is — '

'Polly! That's enough!'

'I'll get you a nice cup of tea, shall I?' she asked soothingly.

Abbie refused to be soothed. 'I do not want a 'nice cup of tea'!' she returned, but was immediately remorseful. It wasn't Polly's fault. She had simply come too close to the truth for comfort. Traipsing about from one dreary flat to the next had forcefully reminded her of all she had lost. No, not lost. Thrown away.

She had been so certain of his love she had been careless of her marriage, taking it for granted, not recognising the danger until it was too late. She had lost not just her beautiful home, she had lost the company, the shared pleasures, the physical presence of Grey in her bed. She suffered the pain of her physical need of him as well as the mental agony of separation.

Abbie dragged her mind back to

present reality; dwelling on the past would only make matters worse. 'What am I saying?' she demanded, trying on a smile that didn't feel very convincing. 'Of course I want a cup of tea. But I'll make it. You must have some project work you should be getting on with.'

'Can I use the computer?'

Abbie grinned at the ease with which the young exploited any sign of weakness. Then, halfway to the kitchen, something occurred to her. If Polly had been to the flat, why hadn't she said anything about Grey, or Emma or the baby? Tact? That wasn't exactly her style. 'Actually, I bought some teacakes yesterday,' she said. 'Perhaps you'd like one before you start work?'

'Oh, great. I'll toast them while you make the tea.'

'So, tell me,' Abbie said as she filled the kettle, 'now you've met him, what did you think of Grey?' she asked.

'Oh, I didn't meet him. He was away all last week.'

'Really?' Relief was short-lived. 'But

if Grey was away, why would Jon take you to the flat?'

'Oh, he told me about the Degas, and as his father has a spare key — '

'Degas?' A jolt like a thousand volts of electricity shot through her.

'The one with the girl bathing . . . I'm doing art history for A-levels.'

'I didn't think Degas figured too prominently in the syllabus, Polly.' She thought of Jon, tall and handsome like his father. Like his uncle. She hated what she was thinking. 'Besides, it was sold months ago.' She turned. 'So, what was the real reason for going to the flat?'

'But the picture was there,' Polly declared. 'I saw it.'

'Did you? Or was it a copy that Jon used to tempt you with?'

'Of course it wasn't a copy. Besides, I didn't need tempting, I wanted to — ' Then she realised what Abbie was implying. 'Oh, Abbie, I wouldn't!' Abbie let out a breath of sheer relief that she hadn't even been aware of holding. Too soon. 'Not sneaking around in someone else's flat while they were away. It would have to be a bit more special than that.'

'It rarely is,' Abbie warned her. But her body taunted her, remembering. With Grey the first time had been special. Every time had been special. Even when he was deceiving you? The voice in her head was scornful. Making love to Emma, then coming home to your bed? How special was that? How could he do that? She turned abruptly from her pale reflection in the dark kitchen window. 'Just make sure you don't find somewhere *special* until your mother comes home,' she said.

'Well, actually, Jon did ask me to go away with him next week. It's half-term.'

'Oh?' Abbie chose not to rise to the bait, fairly certain that this was just in the nature of a wind-up — Polly's retaliation for her leap to the wrong conclusion. 'Where did he have in mind? Paris is always romantic . . . but cold in February. Rome, perhaps? That would fit in with the art history. Or somewhere warmer? That's probably best if you've only got a week. You won't have to waste so much time taking off your clothes.'

A satisfactory blush darkened Polly's cheeks, but she pressed on. 'What would you do if I said I wanted to go?'

'Call your mother to see if she minded?' Abbie offered.

'In that case there's no point in asking.'

The answer was somehow disingenuous. 'If you were thinking of going without permission, Polly, I warn you that I would be forced to call Jon's father and have you both hauled back. The newspapers would greatly enjoy the spectacle. I doubt if you would find it so much fun to have your photograph plastered all over the front pages, and Jon would be back at boarding school before his feet could touch the ground. I'll leave your mother's reaction to your imagination.'

'Jon's father is away next week,' Polly informed her, with an infuriatingly innocent expression.

'Are those teacakes burning?' The cups rattled against the saucers as Abbie began to lay a tray.

'So you'd have to call Grey instead.'

Abbie lifted her head from her task and met Polly's eye. 'Another word on the subject, Polly, and I promise you will spend your entire half-term chained to my wrist.'

⋆　⋆　⋆

The trouble was, Abbie thought, as she struggled with Margaret's ancient Mini in the driving rain, that interlaced with Polly's madcap romanticism was a steely strand of common sense. And that had completely fooled her into believing that she would never actually do anything so thoughtless, so irresponsible, so downright stupid as taking Jon up on his offer.

Abbie could have kicked herself. If

Polly hadn't mentioned Grey she might have probed a little deeper into the girl's intentions, and she might then have been able to persuade her that it would be wiser to keep her passion on hold until after her A-levels.

It was just luck that Abbie had been able to work out where the wretched pair had gone. Young Romeo wasn't taking his Juliet somewhere sophisticated. And they would need more than love to keep them warm. But it was secret. And it was special. She knew, because she had been there often enough herself. With Grey.

And the day had started with such promise. Details of the perfect flat had arrived in the post, and also a note from Steve Morley, asking her to call at the office to discuss a commission.

Polly, curled up in an armchair by the fire, her revision text at her elbow, had virtuously declined an outing even when offered lunch out, barely lifting her head from Thomas Hardy to wish her luck with the flat. Abbie had left her without a qualm.

The flat had been the first disappointment. It *could* have been perfect. But it had needed far more than the coat of paint the agent had suggested to make it habitable and she didn't have the money to put it right. Although Steve Morley was doing his best to give it to her.

He was offering money, a lot of it, for an exposé on her brother-in-law and his phoney marriage. He seemed to think that now Abbie had split with Grey her loyalty was no longer an issue. When she had made it clear that he was mistaken he had suggested that work might not be so forthcoming as it had been in the past. It hadn't been very subtle, but when she had told him what she thought of him she hadn't been particularly subtle either.

When finally, soaked to the skin and thoroughly miserable, she had arrived home, it had been to find a letter from her solicitor enclosing papers to be signed to end her marriage. She'd stuffed them in her bag, not wanting Polly to see. It was then that she had realised Polly hadn't come bounding out of the living room to ask her about the flat.

'Polly,' she'd called, going through into the kitchen. Polly hadn't been there, but had thoughtfully left her a message on the small chalkboard.

Decided that Jon's week of passion sounded more fun than revising. Don't worry about a thing, Abbie. I promise we'll be back in time for school on Monday. Love, Polly.

*Don't worry!* 'Oh, Polly! How could you do this to me?' she'd demanded out loud, but the empty house had offered no answer. Only the blinking light on the answering machine had held out any hope.

She'd pressed the playback button, half expecting it to be some teenage rag and that Polly's familiar laughing voice would shout 'Got you!' down the line.

The voice was familiar. The warm, rich tones were achingly, heart-searingly familiar. But it hadn't been Polly.

'My name is Grey Lockwood. My nephew Jon left this number as a contact for half-term. Could you ask him to call me? It's quite urgent as he seems to have taken the keys to my holiday cottage . . . '

As shock had buckled her legs Abbie had swayed and clutched at the newel post, kept herself upright, although she could hardly have said how. The holiday cottage. Ty Bach. That was where they had gone.

# 5

Abbie had stopped only to pack an overnight bag before backing Margaret's car out of the garage and switching on the radio to get the traffic and weather reports. The radio had hissed uncooperatively at her, and it had quickly become obvious that the little Mini, used mostly for shopping trips, was in no condition for a two-hundred-and-fifty mile dash down a busy motorway. But it was all she had, so she had gritted her teeth in the face of the weather and rush hour traffic, drastically revising her estimate of the time the journey would take.

A dark Mercedes cruised past her now, in the centre lane. A superbly crafted, highly tuned Mercedes 500 SL, exactly like the one that Grey drove, although the colour was impossible to make out in the dark. In *Grey's* car the journey took four hours, she thought grimly. If she had taken Polly's advice and rung him, she might even now be cruising along the motorway in comfort at a steady seventy miles an hour. But comfort would have been a high price to pay for asking for his help. Too high. And this way, with luck, they would all be back home by lunchtime tomorrow without him ever knowing of her involvement.

Beyond the Severn Bridge the rain turned sleety, sticking to the windscreen, and she thought then that it was as bad as it could get. But just after she left the motorway it began to snow.

Despite her aching muscles and the weirdly hypnotic quality of the snowflakes whirling towards her, thicker and thicker in the headlights, Abbie kept her foot firmly on the accelerator until she turned off the dual carriageway to run down beside the Afon Tywi to the coast. Squinting into a darkness so dense that it could almost be cut with a knife, she only just saw the left fork in time, and the squishy noise of the tyres on the road suddenly quietened as she turned onto a narrow and undulating lane that hadn't borne traffic since the snow had begun to fall.

She was moving slowly now, second gear slow, looking for the stunted oak that marked the almost hidden turning, but her headlights, reflected blindingly by the snow, reached only a few feet in front of her.

Afraid that she had missed it, Abbie gave an audible cry of relief when she saw the tree, its branches and trunk plastered with driving snow so that the stark outline was blurred. She jammed her foot on the brake and locked the wheels.

The lane sloped steeply, terminating on the rock-strewn beach a few hundred feet from the turning, and the car continued to slide towards it, completely unresponsive to the wheel, for what seemed like a lifetime. But it couldn't last, and as the lane took a sudden sidestep to the left the car continued straight on towards the hedge.

Abbie's relief that there was something to stop her before she slid, unchecked, into the freezing waters of Carmarthen Bay was rudely shattered as the offside front wheel hit the ditch and the car was caught and spun by its impetus until it was facing in the opposite direction. Then the rear wheel followed its partner and the car slipped sideways, tipping over with a rending of metal and glass that seemed wholly alien in that white and silent world.

For a moment Abbie remained very still, hanging in her seat belt against the door and feeling oddly elated that she had survived without so much as a scratch. Then the lights went out, and it took all her self-control to bite back a scream. Forcing her trembling fingers to unhook the seat belt, she clambered on equally shaky legs over the passenger seat and out of the car.

She stood for a moment, shivering with more than cold in the driving snow, although her short thick coat did little enough to protect legs inadequately covered by a flirty little skirt that lifted eagerly to the wind. Suitable for a London creeping towards spring. Hardly appropriate for a blizzard. And her boots — fine, supple black leather that rose elegantly to her knees — had been made for city streets. She had come rushing into Wales hot on the heels of a pair of amorous teenagers; she hadn't had time to listen to the weather forecast.

She grabbed her bag and, pulling her collar up around her neck, turned her face to the wind, her leather soles slipping on the steep surface as she began the hard trek to the cottage. The biting wind that howled under her skirt mocked the flimsy protection of her tights and found every inch of bare skin at wrists and neck. Snowflakes slammed into her face, and the steep, slippery track that led to the cottage rapidly drained every ounce of adrenalin-charged energy from her legs.

Head down, she dug her feet in and kept going, step after wrenching step, until she felt as if she had been walking for hours. If only she'd had some kind of beacon to guide her it would have been easier to judge her progress, take encouragement as she neared her goal. She raised her weary head and strained to see through the blizzard, and just for a moment she imagined that she saw a light flickering ahead of her.

She blinked the snow from her lashes and it disappeared. Had she imagined it? Or had it just been some distant headlight, twisting and dipping on a road miles away? She wrapped her collar tighter round her neck in an effort to keep out the insinuating snow-flakes, but then, tempted to look again, she caught another glimmer that seemed tantalisingly closer.

'Jon?' Her voice made no impact against the wind, barely escaping from her mouth. 'Jon!' Suddenly she panicked and, dropping her bag, she tried to run. Tried to reach that elusive little light before it disappeared again. That was when she missed the path and stepped into a drift that seemed to open up and swallow her.

The snow crept in everywhere. Inside her coat, filling her skirt and moulding about her thighs — not that she could feel them any more. It filled her mouth too, and her ears and her nose. Oddly, it wasn't cold, just unbelievably peaceful, lying there wrapped in a snowy blanket after the nightmare of battling against the wind. Too peaceful. Abbie knew that if she didn't get up she would go to sleep where she lay. The kind of sleep from which she would never wake up. And she mustn't let that happen. It was vital that she get up and carry on. For Polly.

'I should have phoned Grey,' she murmured. 'He would have known what to do. He always knows what to do.' And then she closed her eyes.

'Wake up!' Someone was shaking her. 'Wake up, damn you!' Although her lids were heavy as lead, and lifting them took more effort than she would have believed possible, the voice was imperative, insistent, so she obeyed. 'Abbie?' She saw the word form on his lips, but the wind whipped the sound away.

'Grey?' Her own lips were too numb to move, let alone make a sound. Not that it mattered, because it couldn't be him. She must be dreaming. Or dead. Maybe that was it. Because the apparition's hair was white, not black, and he was wearing some strange white garment. She was dead, she decided, and in her own special hell where the angels all had Grey's face. And that really was too cruel. She might have been careless of his love, but she wasn't the one who had cheated, and she didn't deserve that kind of hell.

So she shut her eyes again, because it was, on the whole, easier than making a formal complaint. She did wonder briefly if angels were allowed to use that kind of language. Then she remembered — he was an angel from hell. A hell's angel. It was encouraging that she was still able to make a joke and she tried to smile, but her face refused to co-operate. Anyway, it really was too much effort.

Her angel, however, had other ideas. He picked her up bodily and dumped her on her feet before giving her a thorough shaking, so that she was forced to put up her arms and defend herself. This show of resistance apparently pleased him.

'That's better,' he said, if a little grimly. 'Now, you're going to have to make some effort to help yourself, Abbie. There's no way I can carry you up the lane.'

She was too big even for angels? 'I've lost weight,' she protested. 'I may be tall, but I'm skinny.' Then, puzzled, 'Can't you fly?' she asked, her frozen lips stumbling over the words. He swore again, but apparently thought better of a repeat shaking, for which she was grateful.

Her gratitude did not last long as he looped his arm around her waist and began to drag her unceremoniously up the hill, slipping and cursing with every step. He fell once with her, pitching headlong into the snow, and she was quite happy to lie there since it was infinitely preferable to the painful jolting. But despite her complaint he refused to leave her there, hauling her back onto her feet, forcing her to continue.

Once she was inside the cottage, she had to admit that it had been worth it. The cottage was warm. At least, it was warm in contrast to the blizzard howling outside, and the glow of the lamplight from the table added to the illusion. But there was no fire in the hearth, and as he dumped her unceremoniously in the centre of the room she began to shiver uncontrollably.

'You'd better get out of those wet clothes while I light the fire,' Grey instructed her, his voice hard and unwelcoming, and Abbie realised that any idea of her rescuer being an angel was an illusion. No angel had ever had that thick dark hair, plastered wet against his head as he shook off the confusing white pelt of snow and pulled off his snow-covered jacket. No angel had those dark eyes, that angry expression.

'I haven't got anything to change into,' she said helplessly, wondering why she was mumbling. Then, because she wasn't helpless, she turned back to the door. 'I dropped my bag. I must get it.'

He moved swiftly across the room to block the way and, catching her arms, steered her back towards the huge black-leaded range that filled the hearth. The fire was already laid, ready for a match, with screws of paper and kindling and a heap of dry logs. There were more logs, logs with snowflakes still clinging to them, lying where they had been dropped untidily by the hearth. Grey struck a match and put a flame to the paper, watching until he was certain that it had properly caught before turning back to her, his face hard and bitter in the dark shadows thrown by the leaping flames.

'For heaven's sake, couldn't you have made some effort?' he demanded.

Then, looking at her more closely, he swore viciously and began to unfasten the buttons of her coat. Without warning her teeth began to chatter uncontrollably, not just from the bitter weather, but from the deep abiding chill that emanated from the man she had renounced so that he could have his heart's desire. Not that she expected him to be grateful, because he didn't know that.

He pulled off her coat and snow scattered everywhere, and he swore once more. It was odd, she thought, he never used to swear at all. Maybe it was the mess she was making on the carpet that was making him so angry. She'd clean up later, if only he'd hurry so that she could feel the warmth of the fire. Sweater, skirt . . . The fiddly buttons of her blouse seemed to cause him problems, but when she tried to help he simply took her hands and put them back by her sides. 'Leave it, I'll be quicker,' he said harshly.

So she stood, shivering in the firelight, trying not to remember the times without number that he had undressed her in the happier past. Slowly sometimes, tormentingly slowly, his hands brushing against her skin, touching her briefly, as if by accident, so that when he had finished she would be almost collapsing with desire. Never with this dreadful, unseeing expression, as if she were a dress shop dummy that he particularly disliked, snatching his hand back from her skin as if it might contaminate him.

As her sodden bra dropped onto the growing pile of her discarded clothing, she instinctively lifted her arms to cover herself, and his mouth twisted in what once might have been a smile but was now a humourless grimace.

'I'm hardly likely to be impressed with false modesty, Abbie,' he said. 'Not after Atlanta.' And he seized her tights and pants and in one movement stripped them down, waiting impatiently for her to lift her feet so that he could pull off her boots and remove this last vestige of covering. 'Can you walk upstairs to bed, or do I have to carry you?' he enquired distantly as he stood up.

She couldn't see his face, or his expression in the shadowy light. 'Just bring me a blanket. I . . . I'll be all right here,' she said, shivering pitifully.

'You always were a difficult patient,' he said, but he didn't bother to argue, simply bending down and scooping her up in his arms.

She opened her eyes wide. 'I'm n-n-not s-sick,' she stammered.

'Just very nearly dead,' he said, with a grimness that convinced. And, satisfied that he had made his point, he carried her up the wide open-tread staircase to the gallery bedroom that cantilevered over the single room of the old Welsh longhouse, pulling back the thick down-filled quilt before dumping her onto the bed and wrapping her up in it.

'C-c-could I have a hot water bottle?' Abbie managed to stammer the words through her chattering teeth.

'The fire's only just lit,' he said harshly. 'It'll be a while before there's enough heat to boil a kettle.'

She was shaking pitifully — frozen, she was certain, to her very bones. But she was not about to get any sympathy from Grey. Stupid to expect any. He had pulled her out of the snow when, from the look of him, he would rather have left her there to die. She should be grateful for that. So she clung to the quilt, curling herself up as small as she could, turning her back on him.

But he had already moved away. She heard his footsteps move from the rug and onto the wooden floor. Well, what had she expected? That he would lie beside her, hold her in his arms and warm her? When he had Emma? She jabbed herself with the thought. How stupid could you get?

It was darker in the gallery, the

flickering firelight and the small glow from the oil lamp downstairs throwing the raftered roof into deep shadows.

She had only been to the cottage once before in winter, not long after they were married, and now it was full of memories, ghosts of the people they had been then, with their lives stretching in front of them. Suddenly, without warning she began to cry. Not noisily — no sob escaped her lips — but with silent tears that poured down her face, scalding hot against her frozen skin.

Then the jar of the bed as Grey sat down beside her warned her that he had not gone far. As she half turned to demand what he was doing, he draped a towel around her head and began to dry her hair.

'I can do that,' she said quickly, lifting her hand from beneath the quilt, but as it collided with his she dropped it rapidly. 'I can do it,' she repeated stubbornly.

'Just stay under the quilt, Abbie, for goodness' sake, and leave it to me.' He didn't sound particularly happy about having to dry her hair, and she supposed that made it all right. Except that his strong hands working at her scalp made her want to weep even more. 'That'll do,' he said abruptly. 'Lie down.'

He tucked the quilt up around her head, but she was facing him now, watching as he briskly rubbed his own hair before tossing the towel back into the tiny bathroom and pulling his sweater and shirt over his head in one single movement. She'd used to get so cross that he didn't undo his buttons before dumping his shirts in the wash. Now the familiar action seemed stupidly endearing. He eased off his shoes and socks and then he stood up, and as she watched from the cocoon of the quilt he shucked off his trousers and briefs and turned to face her.

'Wh-what are y-you doing?' she demanded as he lifted the quilt and eased himself beneath it.

'You're cold, Abbie. It'll be hours

before there's enough hot water to do the job, so I'm very much afraid I'm going to have to warm you myself.'

'No!' A moment ago she had been mentally berating him for not doing just that, but now the word was a long, anguished cry, wrenched from her throat.

'You weren't so reluctant when we last met,' he said, his voice like ice. But his skin was unbelievably warm as he looped his arm beneath her and pulled her hard against his body, lifting her still-damp hair from her neck. 'What was it you offered? One last whirl for old times' sake . . . ? Now might be a good time.'

She tried to jerk free of his arm, but his grip was painfully strong. 'Let go of me!' she demanded. How dared he touch her? How dared he presume . . . ? But with his free hand he was already rubbing fiercely at her calves, heating her frozen flesh until the feeling began to come back with an agonising rush of pins and needles. As she groaned his hand moved higher, along her thighs, all the time massaging life into her body.

He turned her over onto her stomach and kneeling over her in the cave he made of the quilt, he began briskly to knead her shoulders, working over her arms, down the smooth indentations of her spine to her buttocks. There was nothing loving, nothing gentle about his attentions, and several times she cried out as his pinching fingers hurt her.

'Stop complaining,' he muttered fiercely. 'My God, woman, have you any idea how lucky you are to be alive? That I happened to be here? Not that it would have made any difference if I hadn't just gone outside to fetch some more logs when your car slid into the ditch. It did slide into the ditch, didn't it?' He seemed to gather some satisfaction from that.

'I . . . d-didn't see the t-tree until the last moment.'

'So you jammed on your brakes. If I hadn't heard the crash . . . '

He paused briefly in his painful ministrations and she turned over to stare up at him, as with a sudden rush of concern, she remembered what she was doing in this nightmare. He stared down at her, lying naked between his legs, her body flushed where it had been pushed into the mattress as he had pummelled the life back into her. She had turned without thinking, but now his eyes, gleaming in the soft glow of the lamp, warned her that she had made a mistake.

'Why *are* you here, Grey?' she demanded quickly, and her words seemed to jolt him out of his ransacking contemplation of her body.

'I have every right to be here,' he said harshly. 'And as it's a family matter I really don't think it's any of your business, do you? Right now, I'm more interested in finding out *your* reasons for snooping around the cottage. Did your boyfriend send you on a scouting mission?'

'Boyfriend?' She repeated the word

faintly, as if she had never heard it before and it had no meaning for her. What on earth did he mean by that?

'Or did you simply sell out to the highest bidder?' She flinched away from him as he began to stroke, more gently now, more dangerously, at her neck, then across her shoulders, his thumbs finding every delicate hollow. But there was no escape from his touch as he straddled her, heating her body with his own. 'What does thirty pieces of silver buy these days?' he demanded.

Oh, she could tell him that. A new kitchen and bathroom, curtains, fitted carpets and gallons of paint ... 'I wouldn't take it,' she said.

'You expect me to believe that?' he demanded.

'It's the truth.'

'You wouldn't recognise the truth if it hit you with a ten-foot pole,' he said. 'You lie with your mouth and you lie with your body.'

'No,' she protested.

'You're lying now. Cringing away

from me, pretending that you don't want me to touch you. But you do, Abbie.' He cradled a breast in the palm of his hand and the nipple leapt to painful attention. 'You're like a junkie in need of a fix, longing for me to touch you — '

'No!'

'Tell the truth, Abbie,' he taunted her. 'How long has it been? Hours? Days?'

Oh, God. Too long. And feeling the heat of his body so close was doing terrible things to her, sapping her will, draining her of everything except the desire to hold him, feel his skin against hers.

'Touch me, Abbie,' he urged. 'If you touch me I won't be able to deny you.'

His voice was breaking up. It was true that he wanted her. In some way that she could not hope to understand he wanted her, with a desperation that reached out to her through the black desire in his eyes. And as his lips touched her throat and the rough, dark hairs of his chest grazed her breasts some primitive response was fired deep within her, and she did as she was told and reached out hungrily for him.

It was as if she had set off a volcanic eruption, not just in Grey, releasing all her own pent-up desires, the battened-down needs that had been smouldering for months beneath the ultra-cool exterior she'd maintained for the outside world. She opened up to him, her frozen body melting under the heat of his passion, the blood racing feverishly through her veins as she met his hunger head-on.

Fierce, direct, without any minor key explorations of each other's desires, it was too intense a conflagration to be long sustained. They crash-dived to oblivion and, exhausted, slept.

★   ★   ★

Abbie woke, deliciously warm and comfortable, a hot water bottle at her back. Turning over, she clutched it to her stomach and buried herself deeper under the quilt. She felt good. Happy. It was a forgotten, almost alien sensation, this happiness, and her eyes flickered open on the day as she tried to work out what she was so happy about.

The light was strange, bouncing off the rafters with a brilliance that wasn't accompanied by sunlight. Her eyes opened wider. Rafters? And then the happiness, that intense feeling of well-being evaporated as the night, the snow, the cold, all came flooding back. And worse, far worse than that — the memory of what she had done with Grey. She knew then that the glorious sense of well-being was a transitory thing, a feeling that would have to be paid for in remorse and self-loathing, and a groan escaped her lips.

At least she was alone in the bed. She had not woken up to his sleeping figure beside her. But he would have to be faced because there were more urgent concerns to be confronted than her shame over her loss of control. Jon and

Polly were out there somewhere. They might be lost, frightened. Or worse, she thought, remembering how she had fallen into the snow and lain there, too weary to make the effort to get up. She gave a little shiver that had nothing to do with the temperature. She would be there still, frozen to death in the snow, if Grey had not been there when she'd needed him.

She sat up and, wrapping the quilt about her, rose to her knees and peered down into the main room. Grey, fully dressed and with a blanket wrapped about him, was stretched out in a chair, asleep in front of the range. Her initial relief that he had not been beside her in the bed evaporated as she realised that he hadn't simply got up to go about the business of clearing snow, or finding her bag, or arranging for her car to be pulled from the ditch.

The fire had burned low enough to betray the fact that he had been there for many hours, that he had chosen to sleep uncomfortably in a chair rather than lie alongside her. Fury bubbled through her veins. She hadn't asked him to make love to her, for heaven's sake! She certainly hadn't wanted him to. Her face flamed as she realised that wasn't entirely true. He had invited her participation, not forced it upon her.

She threw back the quilt and strode into the bathroom. The water was just warm enough, and she scrubbed her body clean of the scent of him, reminding herself forcibly that she had done nothing to be ashamed of. She was the one who had been betrayed.

Her husband had brought Emma to this cottage, shared this shower with her, slept with her in the same bed, given her a child. Then last night . . . The rat! How could he have made love to *her*? In the same bed? No, not love. It was sex, lust — nothing more. *How could he?* Wasn't one woman at a time enough for him any more? Had it ever been?

She flung open the cupboard door, hoping that the clothes she had left on her last visit would still be there. But her clothes had gone — cleared out to make room for the new occupants in his life. Room for the folding cot, the packs of disposable nappies and all the other paraphernalia that went with child-rearing. All the evidence of his betrayal.

Angry tears stung at her lids as she picked up a thick checked work-shirt that she had bought for him at the market the last time they had come to the cottage. The musky scent of him clung to the cloth, assailing her senses, weakening her fury as she remembered him cutting logs for the fire. She had watched him, admiring the economy of effort with which he had worked, the strength of his shoulders. Painful thoughts, dangerous thoughts and she pushed them away — furiously away. Lust was no substitute for love.

She dressed quickly, clambering into the over-large clothes, cinching in the waist of a pair of Grey's jeans with a belt, rolling up the legs. She found a pair of white woollen socks normally worn inside wellington boots. Well, that was fine. There were always heaps of wellingtons in the scullery and she would be needing a pair, because she certainly wasn't staying at Ty Bach a moment longer than necessary.

She made her way down the stairs to discover that Grey was still asleep. Her lips tightened, but she told herself that she didn't care one way or another as she braved the chill of the scullery to find some outdoor clothes. Five minutes later, warmly covered in a padded gilet, scarf, a heavy waxed jacket and wellington boots, she stomped back into the main room.

Grey had moved, shifted in the chair, and now his head was propped on his hand. He had always been able to sleep on a clothesline, but his relaxed and peaceful posture when so much needed to be done added insult to injury.

Angrily she swept away the arm propping up his head and he shot forward in the chair, waking a fraction before cracking his head on the wooden arm. 'What the . . . ?'

'Your early-morning alarm call, sir,' Abbie said, with a syrupy sweetness that belied the look in her eyes.

Grey regarded her sourly. 'Has anyone ever told you that your technique could do with a little work?' he said.

'My technique, Grey Lockwood, is none of your business. We're all but divorced. But, since you've brought it up, I've got one or two complaints of my own. When you force yourself into somebody's bed and have sex with them, the very least you can do is stick around until they wake up so that you can apologise!'

# 6

'Apologise!' He was wide awake now and on his feet, towering over her. 'Apologise?' he repeated, in utter disbelief. 'For what? Saving your life?'

She blushed but remained defiant. 'You might have saved my life when you dragged me in from the snow,' she declared. 'The rest was . . . unnecessary.'

'You think so? Have you never heard of hypothermia?'

She bridled. 'Of course I have. You're supposed to wrap the victims in aluminium foil and blankets, give them warm drinks — '

'Oh, *are* you? Well, since I had neither, I did the best I could. I didn't realise I was expected to stick around in case you felt the need of a second application of the treatment.'

She shrank back, her face scarlet, her

whole body blushing. Was that what last night had been about? First aid? Her mind suddenly cleared and she remembered with horrifyingly vivid recall just what it was he had said to her. 'If you touch me, I won't be able to deny you . . . ' Had it been that difficult to make himself do what he'd thought necessary?

'I can assure you, Grey, that I haven't the slightest wish to put you to so much trouble.'

'Then, fetching as you look, swaddled up like a home counties mummy, I suggest you take off those outdoor clothes and think about making some breakfast.'

She glared at him. 'Make your own damned breakfast,' she said. 'I've got more important things to do.' She moved across to the door but he beat her to it, cutting off her escape.

'Like what? Rescuing your bag from the snow?'

She refused even to answer such a stupid question, but glared up at him, her eyes huge and dark in her pale face. His fingers brushed against her cheek. A touch so familiar, so longed for, that even now, in this appalling situation, she felt a tremor of some dark longing jar into life.

'I admit you could certainly do with some lipstick, but since you've already indicated a disinclination for my home-made treatment for hypothermia,' he said bitterly, 'you're going to have to put it off for a while.'

His voice jerked her back to reality. 'I . . . I'm walking down to the village to arrange for some transport out of here. You might not be worried about what has happened to Jon and Polly . . . ' Although his apparent lack of concern did surprise her. 'Well, Jon's a boy. And boys are expected to be boys, so I can't really expect you to work up much of a sweat about it, but Polly is my responsibility and I can't just forget it because of a minor snowfall.'

His eyes gleamed dangerously, but his voice was cool enough. 'Who,' he demanded, 'is Polly?'

'She's Jon's girlfriend. Didn't you know? I expected to find them here. That's why I came — '

'So.' A long breath escaped him. 'That's what you're doing here.' His voice hadn't changed much, just enough to warn her that she had said something to anger him. 'You journalists don't miss a trick, do you? I didn't think even Morley would stoop to putting a trail on young Jon as well.' As well? 'But why not? And who else would he send to ferret out such a juicy story? Because you know all the family secrets, don't you? Well, Miss Feature Writer of the Year, as you can see, the birds have flown. No story. No fee.'

Grey's insults flew over her head. She hadn't wanted the stupid award; she hadn't even bothered to fly back from the States to pick it up at the special dinner.

'For goodness' sake, Grey, can't you forget about me for a moment?'

His eyes were cold. 'I've tried, Abbie.

God knows I've tried. But you get under a man's skin.'

She pulled back, stunned by the bitterness in his voice. 'I didn't mean . . . ' No. She had to keep it impersonal. If he and his new love were not as happy as he thought they should be it was none of her business. None. 'We should be getting on to the police, the hospitals,' she urged. 'They might have had an accident.'

'I very much doubt it. Jon at least has been here, but whether he had company I couldn't say — although the fridge is stocked, the freezer too. And, fortunately for you, the bed was made. Domestic touches that Jon would normally overlook.'

'Did they . . . ?'

'No, Abbie, they didn't stop to use it.'

She felt the colour heat her cheeks, but refused to be drawn back down that track. 'Then where are they?' she demanded.

He shrugged. 'I have no idea. They lit a fire but the ashes were cold. They were gone long before I arrived.'

'I've got to try and find them,' she said, moving towards the door.

'Isn't that a bit like shutting the stable door after the filly has bolted?' he asked.

She refused to rise to his somewhat trenchant wit. 'Maybe, but Polly should be revising for her A levels — and I'll have to face her mother when she comes home.'

'That should be an interesting conversation.'

'You're very welcome to come along. Margaret still thinks of Polly as her baby. Jon might just need your protection.'

'Oh, for heaven's sake,' he said, losing patience. 'Aren't you getting this out of proportion? If she's on the brink of her A-levels she must be eighteen, or as near as damn it. And eighteen-year-old virgins are about as rare as hen's teeth.'

'I bow to your wider experience in these matters, although I don't much appreciate being compared to a hen's tooth,' she said, and had the grim pleasure of seeing a dark flush sear his cheekbones. 'However, I can assure you that Polly also falls into that unusual category, so, if you'll let me by, I'd like to try and make certain that what undoubtedly began as a dream for her does not degenerate into a nightmare.'

'Since they have planned this escapade with such care, I imagine that particular aspect of it has not been left to chance,' Grey remarked, with what Abbie considered under the circumstances to be an unforgivably casual attitude to the situation.

'And that makes it all right?'

'No, and Jon will have to answer for his behaviour to his father, but in the meantime — '

'In the meantime?' Abbie interrupted in sheer disbelief, angrier than she would have thought possible. The Grey Lockwood she'd known and loved would never just have sat back and ignored the situation. 'In the meantime I'm supposed to forget it? What on earth has happened to you, Grey?'

Grey stared at her for a moment, and then continued as if she had not spoken. 'In the meantime,' he repeated, 'since there's absolutely nothing you can do about the situation, I suggest you take off your coat and make yourself comfortable. You're not going anywhere, Abbie.'

'You're planning to stop me?' Abbie flared up at him. 'I don't think so.'

As she moved to push past him the left corner of his mouth lifted his face into a sardonic smile, and he raised his hands in a gesture of surrender. 'I wouldn't dream of trying.' And he finally stood aside, offering her the door. 'Help yourself.'

She hesitated for a moment, surprised at this sudden capitulation. Then she shrugged, walking by him with all the dignity her bundled, booted body could manage, and lifted the latch. It was immediately wrenched from her fingers as the door was flung aside and she was enveloped in a white maelstrom of snowflakes that plastered themselves to her face, her boots, the front of her coat. She could see nothing. The world was wiped out, obliterated by a blizzard that sucked the very breath from her body. A white-out.

Grey caught her arm, hauling her back into the safety of the cottage, and by putting his shoulder to the door managed to shut it against the fierce blast. Then, with his back still pressed hard against it, he dropped the latch, and as he looked down at her his mouth finally twisted into a full-blooded grin.

'What's the matter, Abbie?' he asked as she fought to regain her breath. 'Changed your mind?'

'It's never been like this before,' she finally gasped.

'You've never seen it like this before,' he corrected her, as he reached down to brush away the snowflakes that clung to her eyelids with the pads of his thumbs. 'I have.'

'But — '

He removed her hat with a distracted

frown and pushed the damp fringe gently back from her forehead. His hands were warm and smelled of woodsmoke. 'You shouldn't get cold again. Come over by the fire.'

'I'm all right, really,' she protested. 'The cottage is warm now.' Too warm, she thought as, ignoring her protest, he propelled her insistently towards the fire.

He unwound the scarf from her neck, shook off the snow and hung it with the hat behind the door. She pulled at the fasteners that held the front of the coat and they popped open. Not quickly enough. Grey had returned and now reached for the ring at the top of the zip. 'I can manage,' she said quickly, and tugged hurriedly at it. It jammed. Why did zips always do that when you were in hurry? she thought furiously as she wrestled with it.

'You'd better leave that to me,' Grey said, and she was forced to stand before him while he untangled a loose thread from the zipper teeth.

'Tell me about the snow,' she said — anything to distract her from the urgent desire to slide her fingers through the dark tousled head just beneath her chin. To be safe, she closed her eyes as well.

'When Robert and I were kids,' he said, concentrating on the zip, 'Mum decided we should all get away from television and the tawdry commercialism of the season and have a genuine, old-fashioned country Christmas.' He paused, apparently expecting some response.

'That sounds . . . nice.'

'Oh, it was.'

'What did you do?' she asked.

'Do?' He stopped fiddling with the zip and she knew he had looked up. Feeling foolish at being caught with her eyes screwed up tight, she opened them. His face was so close that she could see the tiny gold flecks that gave his eyes that special depth, that special warmth. All illusion, of course. A trick of nature. It meant nothing.

'Without the television,' she said quickly. 'I mean, there isn't a piano to stand around. Isn't that what people always say they used to do in the good old days before television?' Her pathetic attempt at a laugh sounded hollow even in her own ears. 'Stand around the piano and sing?'

'Oh, right. No piano. We had to make do with the wind-up gramophone. You do remember the wind-up gramophone, Abbie?'

She swallowed. Oh, yes, she remembered. Invented in the days when young men had come courting their sweethearts in the front parlour. The playing of gramophone records had been the perfect way for parents to be certain that propriety was being observed, since the machine had to be constantly wound up. One wet afternoon they had found it in the cupboard, and Grey had most memorably demonstrated how a bright youth could buck the system with a little co-operation from his girl.

'Yes, I remember,' she said bleakly,

wondering if he had demonstrated the same technique for Emma.

Apparently satisfied with having made her thoroughly miserable, he returned to the zip and continued with his story. 'We spent the first day cutting up logs and collecting a tree from a nearby farm while Mother got to grips with baking on the range. We visited all the local farmers, saw the first new lambs, went to chapel on Christmas morning. We even played cricket on the beach on Boxing Day . . . ' His voice died away as he dwelt on the memory.

'It sounds wonderful,' Abbie prompted dully.

'It was. I always planned to do it again when — ' He stopped, ran the freed zipper down. Then, as he straightened, he forced a careless shrug. 'Well, some day.'

When he had a family of his own? She reached out as if to touch his arm, pulled back. 'But what about the snow?' she said quickly.

'Snow?' He seemed to have forgotten

the point of his story. 'Oh, yes.' He dropped his eyes from the hand that had so nearly touched him. 'The snow.' He turned to the fire, raking it through, throwing on some logs so that it burst into flaming life, before placing the kettle on the hob. 'That was the only tiny disappointment,' he said as he worked. 'The lack of snow.

'Then, the day before we were due to come home, we had a flurry. Not much, just enough to be fun. We spent our last day making snowmen, eating mince pies, finishing up the milk with mugs of hot chocolate to go with the dripping toast for supper. The perfect end to a perfect holiday.' He straightened, smiled briefly at a distant memory full of warmth and love.

'Then overnight the wind shifted to the north-east and the flurry turned to a blizzard. We were stuck here for three days, eking out the remains of the Christmas feast and with nothing but dried milk powder for the tea. After the second day we ran out of paraffin for the lamps and were reduced to candles. Mother refused ever to come down here again at Christmas, no matter how much Robert and I begged her. After that experience, she said, television and tawdry would suit her just fine.'

'I wish I'd known her.'

'I think I would have spared her that particular pain.' His eyes hardened as the colour drained from her face. 'She was the sort of woman who believed that vows were meant to be kept, that marriage was for ever.'

'Then she was singularly unlucky with both of her sons,' Abbie retaliated, and then clapped her hand over her mouth. She wasn't supposed to know that he had been unfaithful.

The gesture did not go unnoticed. 'Yes, Abbie, a little restraint on that eager tongue of yours might be no bad thing, since we're imprisoned here together for the duration.'

'It would be so much easier if we were strangers,' she said bleakly.

'Infinitely,' he agreed, with feeling.

'We could be very British about the whole thing, very stiff-upper-lip, never straying into the personal . . . ' The idea appeared to offer him some wry amusement. 'Perhaps we should try it? Pretend we've never met. What do you say?' He held out his hand. 'Pax?' he offered. 'For the duration.'

His hands were beautiful. Large, square, with long, fine fingers that knew every secret of her responsive body . . .

*No!* No. She mustn't think about it. She must take his hand as if she had never seen it before. Slowly, reluctantly, she raised her own and he closed his fingers about hers. 'Pax,' she agreed, her voice barely audible. Then, because suddenly the air was so thick with tension that you could have bounced a breeze block off it, she said, 'But I do hope there's a decent supply of paraffin this time. And food.'

'I'll have to check the can next time I battle my way across to the barn. At least there's a good supply of fuel. That at least hasn't changed.'

'Oh, Grey!' she said, because so many other things *had* changed. And then, because that wasn't a good start to their resolution, she straightened her shoulders. 'And since there's no hope of getting to my bag, I suppose I'll just have to try and keep my upper lip stiff without the aid of lipstick.'

'Tough,' Grey said, but he had recognised the spirit that allowed her to poke a little fun at herself, and there was a tinge of humour in his voice that robbed the word of its sting. 'So. We'd better be businesslike about this and check to see what we've got to live on for the next few days. I don't know which of the runaways we've got to thank for the provisions — Jon or . . . What did you say her name was?'

'Polly,' she said. It hadn't occurred to her that Grey might never have heard of her. Presumably he didn't know that they had been making themselves at home in his flat while he was away either. She glanced up, and as she met the sudden angry glitter in Grey's eyes decided it might be as well to keep that bit of information to herself. 'What is it?'

He shook his head. 'I just find it hard to believe that you actually went out of your way to get to know an innocent teenage girl in order to get a story. Has Steve Morley really dragged you down that far?'

She sighed. So much for being strangers. 'Grey, although I have to admit that right at this minute I could cheerfully throttle Jon, he is your problem — but Polly happens to be the daughter of a friend. I'm supposed to be looking after her for a couple of months. Obviously I have a lot to learn about the deviousness of teenage girls. Now, do you think you could stop parading your prejudices and give some thought as to how we are going to find them and get the pair of them home?' Then she frowned. 'That is why you're here, isn't it?'

Grey regarded her with considerable suspicion, but she refused to back down from that watchful scrutiny and eventually he lifted his shoulders in the smallest shrug.

'Yes, that's why I'm here. Robert's in America and I thought I'd bring Jon down here for half-term. But first I discovered the cottage keys were missing. Then I couldn't get an answer from the number Jon left . . . and Robert's housekeeper had a rather odd phone call from someone who said she was a journalist asking if it was true that Jon had taken a girl down to the family cottage . . . I thought perhaps I'd better get them out of the way before they made the front page . . .'

Abbie frowned. 'Journalists don't advertise themselves when they're after that kind of story, Grey.'

'Don't they? Well, I suppose you would know. Whatever. They certainly didn't cover their tracks very well.'

'No.' Like his uncle, she thought, as a lump rose unbidden to her throat. 'Actually I did hear your telephone message. That's why I guessed they had come here. How did you get in, if Jon had the keys?'

'He very kindly left them under the mat. If you heard my message, why didn't you phone me, Abbie?'

And risk Emma answering? 'I . . . I thought I could handle it. Unfortunately I didn't hear the weather forecast before I set out, and the car radio wasn't working . . . ' She gave an involuntary little sniff as her attempt to be cool wobbled a little, and Grey thrust a handkerchief into her hand. 'I think I must have caught a cold last night.'

'You don't catch a cold from lying in the snow, Abbie. You get pneumonia.'

'Do you? You always did know things like that. Didn't you do a first-aid course once?'

'I went to a session on emergency procedures after I had a witness collapse in court,' he corrected her.

'I expect that's how you learned the best way to treat hypothermia. Did the instructor demonstrate the technique . . . ?' His face drained of colour.

How could she have said that? How *could* she?

'I never said it was the best way. I just read something once . . . I can't remember where . . .'

'Forget it!'

'Easier said than done,' he replied. 'I have a retentive memory. In fact, last night — '

'As I was saying,' Abbie said sharply, firmly slamming the door on the subject of last night, 'I thought I could handle it. As you said, it wasn't difficult to work out where they were heading.'

'No. Not difficult. But she's young. With you looking after her I'm sure she'll soon learn to manage things better,' he remarked bitterly.

'That's unfair!' she blazed at him, the words out before she could recall them. Of course it was fair, she reminded herself, quickly retreating from the challenge, dropping her eyes. He only thought what she had wanted him to think. It was ridiculous to get angry because she had done her job so well.

She managed a shrug, as if after all it didn't matter. 'The trouble is, I thought that Polly was winding me up — teasing me. She's pretty good at that. But when I got back from seeing Steve last night . . . ' She faltered as his eyes narrowed dangerously at Steve's name, but he did not pursue it. 'When I got back from my meeting,' she continued, more carefully, 'I was confronted with a message informing me that she and Jon intended to pursue a week of passion in order to break up the monotony of A-level revision — '

'She actually wrote that?' he demanded, shocked out of his scornful posture.

'Polly is somewhat direct. She also promised they would be back in time for school on Monday. I'm sure she meant it, but I find it very difficult to believe that she thought I would just leave it at that — '

'Tell me about Polly,' he interrupted.

'She's bright, bubbly and great company. I'm not surprised Jon fell for her.'

'I wasn't asking for a reference. I

meant your connection. What is your connection with her?' The hard lines of his face suggested that he was still not entirely convinced that she wasn't simply out on a story.

'I told you, I'm keeping an eye on her for a friend. No one you've ever met.'

'I can believe that,' he said, his voice heavy with meaning.

'Polly's *mother*,' Abbie said. 'Margaret was a mature student when I was at college. Her husband is a botanist and she wanted to take photographs for him. They spent the last few years in Australia . . . ' His expression told her that he wasn't interested in the occupation of Polly's father or her mother's desire to help him. 'We lost touch. They were moving about a lot and I was busy. It's so easy to let things slip away from you . . . ' She snapped herself back to the matter in hand. 'They came home about a year ago, and Margaret wrote to me at the paper when I received the award.'

'How very touching.'

She ignored his sarcasm, telling herself that it didn't hurt — at least no more than a splinter under a nail. 'Her older daughter married an Australian and still lives out there. She . . . she's just had a baby. Margaret gave me a roof over my head when I came home, and keeping an eye on Polly while she visited her new grandson seemed the least I could do — ' His exclamation of disgust cut her short. 'What's that supposed to mean?' she demanded, at last snapping under his barrage of abuse.

But, having driven her to lose control, Grey finally relaxed, rewarding himself with the faintest of smiles. 'It means, my dear, that anyone who leaves a teenage girl in your care deserves everything they get.' The sudden whine of the kettle as it began to boil cut off her furious reply. 'I think that's your cue to make some breakfast,' he said.

'And what are you going to do? Sit there and watch me?' she threw at him.

'How could any man resist an invitation couched in such tender terms?'

'Try,' she instructed. 'Very hard.'

'Well, you always did say I got under your feet,' he said. 'But then, you do have very large feet.'

'Long,' she corrected automatically. She had long, narrow feet. Too late she saw the glint in his eye.

'Some things never change. The vanity of women is as unfailing as the tides. Although why you should be so sensitive about your feet beats me,' he said, retreating into the scullery. 'I mean, you're tall — you need them for balance . . .'

It was an old taunt with a time-honoured response. But Abbie caught herself as she cast about her for something to throw. That kind of row only had one possible ending. Surely Grey, with his retentive memory, knew that as well as she did?

'All right! I admit it, they're large,' she called after him. 'Huge. Positively flipper-sized feet. Does that make you happy . . . ?' The words died on her lips as he reappeared, clad in a jacket and boots. 'You're not going out in this weather?' she demanded, shocked out of her couldn't-care-less response.

'I have to. We need more logs,' he said. 'But don't fret. If I don't make it, you'll be a rich widow instead of a penniless divorcee.'

'What a perfectly beastly thing to say,' she retaliated. 'Do you think I would take a penny from you? Emma and Matthew — '

His face registered blank shock. 'You *know* about Emma?'

She should take her large feet and stick them in her large mouth, but it was too late to call the words back, to pretend any more. 'Yes,' she admitted. 'I know.'

'And Matthew? I suppose Morley told you?'

Anything was better than confessing to witnessing that scene in the park. And it was near enough to the truth. 'Yes,' she said. 'He saw you having lunch with her.'

He frowned. 'But that was months

ago. Before — before you left.' He regarded her with sharp, penetrating eyes that sought out her secrets. 'Have you known that long?' She nodded. 'Morley too?' She nodded again. 'Then why didn't he use it? I mean, once I'd hit him he had the perfect opportunity to bring the whole messy business out into the open.'

'I asked him not to, Grey.'

His head flew back as if she had struck him and pain, real pain, creased his eyes. 'He did that for you?' His reaction was unexpected. He should have been pleased, for heaven's sake, but he looked angry. 'I didn't think the man capable of . . . of loving anyone enough to suppress a story that big. And I was blindly taking you for granted, so wrapped up in my own problems that I couldn't see. I suppose I got what any careless lover deserves.'

'You were never that, Grey.'

'No?' He raised his hand and very briefly touched her cheek. 'I must have been doing something wrong.' He reached for the latch, but turned back to her. 'When I walked out of that motel room in Atlanta, Abbie, I really wanted to believe your lies. It was so much easier to think that you had changed overnight from the girl I took to my bed, when I discovered to my joy that I was her first lover. It was so much easier than acknowledging that you had fallen in love with someone else, that you would have done anything to get me out of that room, said anything to protect Steve Morley. I should have known better.'

And with that he opened the door and disappeared into the blizzard driving across the yard.

# 7

Abbie struggled to close the door behind him, battling against the fierceness of the wind. Finally it was done, the wild elements shut out along with Grey. Leaning weakly against it, she lifted her hand to where the touch of his fingers still burned against her cheek, wet from the snow and the warmer touch of tears.

She didn't know how she was going to bear it. Being stranded at the cottage with Grey was like something from her worst nightmare — a nightmare in which she was forced to relive every moment they had ever spent there together.

She had surrendered her own happiness so that he could begin again with his new love. But something had gone wrong. Badly wrong. Because he wasn't happy. It didn't take any kind of a genius to see that. She wanted to hold him, to cradle him in her arms and tell him that it didn't matter. But it did. He had betrayed her, and last night he had betrayed Emma too. There was no way back for either of them.

But life continued, and when he returned he would be cold and hungry. If she couldn't tell him that she loved him, she could at least provide him with more substantial succour.

When he burst in through the door, arms full of logs, she was bending over a pan of bacon. He dropped the wood beside the hearth with a clatter that made her jump. 'This is quite like old times,' he said, straightening. 'Apart from the snow.'

She flinched. Too much like. But as she turned and handed him a mug of tea she managed to meet his eyes. 'Apart from a lot of things. I thought we had an agreement, Grey, that this would be a lot easier if we pretended to be strangers.'

'The trouble is, Abbie, I don't want it

to be easy for you. I want you to hurt as much as me.'

'Hurt! You've got some kind of nerve, Grey Lockwood,' she declared hotly. 'After what you've done . . . '

He looked at her as if she was crazy. 'And what precisely have I done?'

Something snapped inside her. 'You've lied to me, cheated, betrayed me . . . ' He was going to deny it, she could see it by the look of stunned disbelief that crossed his features. 'I offer in evidence a non-existent case conference in Manchester,' she threw at him, 'when in fact you were here all the time. With Emma.' That stopped him in his tracks.

'I was protecting you — ' he began.

'By lying to me?'

He tilted his head back, looked somewhere over her head. 'Yes. By lying to you. At the time I thought it was for the best.' He turned away. 'But clearly you didn't want to be protected. At least, not by me.' He shrugged out of his coat and hung it behind the door. 'My mistake.' When he turned back to face her, his eyes had hardened to stone. 'You're right, Abbie. We are strangers. The girl I married would never have hurt anyone.'

'I trusted you, Grey. I would have trusted you with my life.'

'Would have?' His jaw tightened ominously. 'Your memory seems to have short-circuited. I thought you just did.'

And with that exchange they might indeed have become total strangers, because breakfast passed without another word between them, and as Abbie rose to clear the plates Grey took himself off to the far side of the room to attend to the fire. The sharp scent of the wood-smoke caught in her throat as she cleared away, making her eyes sting. What other reason could there possibly be for the tears that washed her eyes? Stupid, ridiculous tears.

Oh, Polly, how could you do this to me? she silently demanded of the absent girl as she watched Grey sink to his haunches to riddle through the ash.

Superbly muscled thighs packed the workmanlike denim of his jeans as he jabbed at the fire, his shoulders stretching the thick flannel shirt. And as the heavy, painful ache of her longing for him sucked the strength from her limbs she fled to the safer discomfort of the freezing scullery and the washing up.

'Have you checked the freezer?' Grey's voice so close behind her made her jump, and the cup she had been about to place on the draining board slithered from her cold fingers and smashed on the stone floor. She quickly bent to pick up the pieces, and in her haste jagged her hand on the sharp edge of the china.

'Still accident-prone,' Grey said as he saw the blood oozing from her finger, and, taking her hand, drew her back to her feet. 'Everything changes, everything stays the same.' He turned and reached for the first-aid box, kept on the shelf above the sink, deftly cleaned the wound and applied a plaster. Then, as he always had, he raised the finger to his lips to kiss it better.

'Don't!' He stepped back sharply at her panic-stricken exclamation and the china crunched beneath his shoe. Stupid! A stupid overreaction to a purely automatic gesture.

'You'd better put something on your feet before you cut something else,' he said, staring at her for a long moment before turning away, fishing a pair of trainers from the pile in the corner. 'Here.'

They were hers, apparently overlooked in the general eradication of her presence from his life. 'Yes. Yes, of course,' she agreed quickly, taking them from him. Anything to stop him looking at her like that. While he swept up the mess she slipped her feet into the shoes and bent to tie the laces.

When she straightened he was bending over the freezer. Come on, Abbie, she urged herself. You can do this. She had to, it was imperative that she keep a grip on her emotions. 'Well, are we going to starve?' she asked, with a cool attempt at humour.

The cottage had no electricity supply and the refrigerator and the large chest freezer were both run on bottled gas. Grey was still leaning over the freezer, regarding its contents with a slightly puzzled expression. 'They've left us pretty well supplied. Is Polly taking domestic science for her A-levels?'

'Polly!' she exclaimed, startled out of her pretence. 'Good grief, no. I've never seen her cook anything but pizzas and bean burgers.'

'Well, it looks as if she was going to play the good little housewife to the hilt for Jon's benefit. Not a convenience package in sight.'

'I don't believe it!' she exclaimed. He stepped aside so that she could see for herself. 'There are even some frozen vegetables,' she said. Polly would do anything rather than eat vegetables. A fact Abbie had always considered rather odd, since she was going through the almost mandatory vegetarian stage of adolescence. 'Does Jon like broccoli? There seems to be rather a lot of it.'

'The only person I know who actually likes frozen broccoli, Abbie, is you.'

'Spinach?' she asked hopefully.

'Likewise.'

'Well. That's me taken care of. And there's cauliflower for you.'

'Only if you make a cheese sauce.'

She opened the fridge door. 'You appear to be in luck. There's no shortage of the stuff.'

'Right, well, what do you fancy for lunch? There's steak and lamb. I don't suppose there's any — '

'Mint?' As she produced a jar from the refrigerator a puzzled frown plucked at her brow. 'It seems you're right. Polly had planned a week of total domesticity. I do hope she had the foresight to provide herself with a cookery book.' She closed the fridge door a touch thoughtfully. The vegetarian phase hadn't lasted for long, it seemed. 'Can you get a loaf out of the freezer while you're there?'

'There isn't one.'

'Oh, great! Trust them to forget the simple things.'

Grey had transferred his attention to the cupboards. 'I don't think they forgot. I think they were planning to do-it-yourself.' He indicated several packs of bread flour and some dried yeast.

It was if someone had struck a bell in her head. She and Polly had been toasting muffins in front of the fire one day, and Polly had been digging away as usual about Grey. To distract her, she had told Polly about the cottage, where everything had to be done on the range — even baking bread if you missed the *barra* man on his rounds. She had extolled the pleasures of breadmaking, she remembered, the rich smell of the dough rising in front of the fire ... Anything to stop herself from thinking about Grey ...

He turned to her now. 'Are you sure they planned a week of passion?' he asked. 'Because frankly I don't think they were likely to have much time for — '

'How long did you say this weather is likely to keep up?' she interrupted shortly.

'I didn't.'

'What about the radio? Can we get a forecast?'

He shook his head. 'The batteries are dead. If I can coincide my next dash across the yard for logs with the news, I'll try the car radio. But that rather depends upon the weather.'

She looked at the flour, took it reluctantly from the cupboard. 'Right. Well, since I've no choice, I suppose I'd better get baking.'

Grey watched as she laid out her ingredients on the table. 'Can I do anything to help?'

'I don't know, Grey. You tell me,' she demanded, looking up at him.

She was angry, but not with him, with herself. She had allowed her longing for Grey to spill over into her new life, talking too much about the past under

Polly's eager prompting. She hadn't even realised she was doing it until now, when it kept coming back to haunt her, because dear, sweet, romantic Polly had thought it would be 'special' to experience that same enclosed intensity that came when you were totally alone with someone you loved.

'If you were really stranded alone with a strange woman,' she asked, 'what would you be doing?'

His mouth twisted in a wry smile. 'That rather depends on the woman.' She supposed she had asked for that, but again it reminded her too forcibly of the kind of remark he would have made in happier days, when they had been certain enough of each other's love to make such jokes. Everything reminded her — every word, every gesture — of a love carelessly lost. He shrugged as she continued to stare wordlessly at him. 'No? Probably not. I'd probably stay as far out of her way as possible.'

She snapped back to reality. 'Then

feel free to do just that,' she invited. 'I won't be offended.'

His eyes taunted her. 'But you're not a stranger, Abbie.'

'Pretend, Grey. It was your idea.' She didn't want him anywhere near her. Nearness hurt. 'And while you're working on that,' she added, 'you might consider the sleeping arrangements for tonight.'

'There's only one bed. And one night in a chair is enough.'

He hadn't spent the entire night in a chair, but she wasn't about to remind him of that. 'You've forgotten that I'm a stranger.' She saw the protest form on his lips and forestalled it. 'A very prim and proper maiden lady who will not expect to share her bed with a man.'

'Oh, yes? And I'm the Archbishop of Canterbury.'

'Not even His Grace,' Abbie returned, doing her best to ignore this attempt to wound.

'In that case she's very welcome to the chair,' he replied, turning away.

'Although I'd advise her to miss out on the wake-up call.' Then he settled himself by the fire, apparently fascinated by an old paperback.

Abbie let out a long, heartfelt breath, and began the slow, soothing process of breadmaking. She heeled the dough, turned it and repeated the action with the same smooth, repetitive movements that had been handed down the centuries. It was quite possible, she thought, as she worked out her tensions on the dough, that if bread were still made by hand in every kitchen, there would be rather less need for tranquillisers.

She put the dough in a clean bowl and, after covering it with a damp cloth, set it to rise near the fire. Grey did not lift his head from the book but moved his feet sideways to give her more room.

'Thank you,' she said stiffly.

'It's no trouble at all.' There was nothing wrong with the words, but she still wanted to hit him.

'Would you like some coffee?' she asked, considering that on the whole it would be wiser to be polite.

'What kind of coffee?'

'You're perfectly safe, Grey, it's not instant.' He finally lifted his eyes from the book, apparently unable to hide his amusement.

'Polly really was trying to impress Jon with her domesticity, wasn't she?' She refused to be drawn on what Polly had been trying to do and he shrugged. 'Coffee will be most acceptable. You'll find the cafetière in the scullery. And since you've got your baker's hat on why don't you make a few Welsh cakes to go with it? It'll help you to pass the time.'

She looked at him in stunned disbelief. 'Make your own damned Welsh cakes,' she flung at him. 'And your own damned coffee too.' And with that she took herself into the scullery to peel potatoes in water that froze the ends of her fingers, although the scalding tears that fell unchecked into the bowl should have made a difference.

'I'm sorry, Abbie. I shouldn't have . . . '

She twitched her shoulder away from his hand. 'It was seeing you kneading the bread, that special smell . . . It was as if the clock had been turned back a year . . . As if everything was as it had always been.'

'Well, it isn't the same!' She turned abruptly to confront him and saw, to her astonishment, that the pain that ate at her was echoed all too plainly in his face, deepening the lines etched into his cheeks.

He reached out, touched her cheek, using his thumb to wipe away the tears. His hands moved, slowly, surely, up to her temples, his fingers splaying out through her hair to cradle her face, lift it to his. 'Don't cry, Abbie,' he murmured softly. And his lips brushed her forehead. 'Please, don't cry.' For a moment they remained perfectly still in the ice box of the scullery, and the silence ran dangerous as a lit fuse between them. Then Grey reached over her and picked up the cafetière. 'I'll make some coffee,' he said. 'You're cold.'

'I'll survive,' she said hoarsely.

'You don't have to act tough with me, Abbie. I know you too well.'

'Do you?' Her challenge died on her lips as she remembered the way he had driven her beyond control the night before. Yes. He knew her far too well for safety. Her scalp still tingled where his fingers had rested moments before. 'If you want something sweet with your coffee why don't you see if the young lovers left us some biscuits,' she said, shakily changing the subject.

She turned back to the sink, aware that for long moments he continued to stare down at her. Then she heard him lift down the biscuit tin and open the lid. 'They thought of everything. Bourbons and . . . ' She heard him bite into something crisp. 'Mmm. Almond Crunch. I wonder which of our lovebirds did the shopping?'

'Jon, probably,' she said, looking round. 'Polly didn't have the time. Why?'

'Nothing. It's just that whoever went to the supermarket seems to have thoughtfully provided us both with our favourite biscuits. That's all.'

★　★　★

Abbie wandered over to the window and rubbed at the glass. 'I think it's easing a bit out there. I can actually see the barn.'

Grey, half asleep in the chair by the fire after lunch, looked up. 'Can you? In that case I'd better go and fetch some more logs while I can.' He stretched and heaved himself to his feet.

'I'll give you a hand,' she offered.

'I can manage.'

'It'll be dark soon. The quicker we work, the better.'

He hesitated for just a second and then shrugged. 'Come on, then. Just make sure you're well wrapped up.'

A few minutes later they were floundering across the yard, up to their knees in soft powdered snow, gasping breathlessly as they reached the shelter of the barn.

'Why don't you try and get the weather on the radio?' she suggested.

Grey glanced at his watch. 'It's too early. Anyway, we know what the weather's doing. Stocking up with fuel while we can is more important.'

She could hardly argue with that, and the two of them staggered back to the cottage with their arms full. They repeated the journey half a dozen more times. 'Stay here, Abbie,' Grey ordered as he turned back for another trip. 'You've done enough.'

'I can keep going as long as you can,' she declared breathlessly.

'Humour me,' he said, and not waiting for her answer he went back out into the snow.

Three more trips and he was beginning to look waxen with the cold. 'Grey, that's enough, surely?' she protested as he dropped the logs in the doorway for her to stack and turned away once more, not bothering to waste his breath on a reply.

By the time she had stacked the logs

neatly along the wall by the hearth he still hadn't returned. She opened the door and peered anxiously into the gathering gloom. It was oddly quiet, and she suddenly realised that the wind had dropped considerably in the last half-hour. But there was something — the faintest distressed cry that raised gooseflesh on her skin. 'Grey?' She strained her ears for his answering call.

This time there was no mistake. But the sound came not from the barn but from the field beyond it. What on earth was he doing there? She had only removed her topcoat and boots and she quickly pulled them back on over the gilet and two pairs of socks. Outside she stopped to listen. Silence. Absolute silence. Away from the lamplight of the cottage, she realised just how dark it had become outside, and a quiver of anxiety feathered her spine.

'Grey?' She heard the sound again, and without stopping to consider the wisdom of her action she plunged into the knee-deep snow and headed in the direction it had come from.

She couldn't open the gate into the field and didn't waste time trying, but climbed over it, plunging into snow up to her thighs and pitching forward as she landed, knocking the wind from her body. But she scrambled quickly to her feet. The sound was nearer, louder — an eerie, wavering cry. And, suddenly realising what it was, she began to dig in the snow with her bare hands.

'Grey!' She raised her voice to heaven, wondering why on earth he didn't answer her. 'There's a ewe buried here. Where are you?' She continued to shout, cursing him with every breath even as she clawed frantically at the snow.

'Abbie!' Relief flooded through her as she finally heard his voice from the yard.

'Over here, in the field.' She saw the jerky movements of the torch as he approached the gate. 'Watch out, it's deeper — ' Too late. The torch described a crazy arc as he tumbled, rolled and cursed as he righted himself.

'What the hell . . . ?' And then he saw for himself as the beam of his torch picked up the head of the ewe. 'Is she alive?'

'Just about. Can you open the gate? We'll never get her over it from this side.'

He didn't stop to discuss the matter but began to work at the frozen metal hoop that held the gate fast, banging at it with his torch until it shifted and he could prise it off the post. Then he handed the battered torch to Abbie, lifted the poor frozen creature from the snow cave made by her body and carried her into the barn.

'What can we do for her?' Abbie asked.

'Rub her with straw. Dry her off.'

'Poor thing,' she said, grabbing a handful of straw and working over the ewe's back.

'It gets worse,' Grey said. 'She's about to drop her lamb.'

Abbie looked up at him in astonishment. 'How can you tell?'

'She's sort of hunched at the rear and she's dropped her head.' He fumbled in his pocket for his car keys and handed them to her. 'Put on the headlights so that I can see properly.'

'What are you going to do?' she asked as he began to strip off his coat and sweater, roll up the sleeves of his shirt.

He looked up into the thin torchlight, his face thrown into dark, chiselled shadows. 'With any luck she'll do it all herself.'

The light from the headlamps bounced off the stone walls, throwing their figures into long, distorted shadows as they hunched over the poor creature, their breath smoking in the freezing air as they watched and waited.

The lamb came surprisingly easily, the delivery over in moments, with just a little help from Grey.

'How do you know about sheep?' Abbie asked as he rubbed the little body with straw, cleaned its mouth and made certain that it was breathing properly.

He looked up briefly. 'There was a time you couldn't keep Robert out of the lambing sheds. He wanted to be a farmer. And at that age, wherever Robert went,' he said, glancing up at her, 'I followed.'

'Robert! A farmer?' The idea of the suave politician bent over the straw, helping a ewe in distress, was even more extraordinary than the sight of Grey now running his hands confidently over the ewe's belly.

His face was thrown into shadows as he looked up. 'There's another one. She's going to need some help.'

'What are you going to do?'

'Deliver it, if I can,' he said, his voice grim as he wrapped the first lamb in his sweater.

'Just tell me what to do — '

'No. I want you to take this one into the warm.' As if sensing the protest forming on her lips, he looked up. 'Now, Abbie, please.' There was no arguing with the determined set of his jaw.

'Right.' She took the tiny creature and, tucking it beneath her coat, hurried through the still, cold night into the warmth of the cottage. He was close behind her, and he put the second lamb with its sibling on the sweater, before heading back to the door. 'Grey? Where's the ewe? Won't she want her lambs?'

'The ewe is dead. Exhaustion.'

He had known it would happen. That was why he had sent her inside. 'Oh, Grey. I'm sorry.'

'It could have been you,' he said angrily. 'Wandering off into the night by yourself like that — I thought you would have learned your lesson . . . ' He caught himself.

'I heard a noise. I — I thought it was you. That you'd fallen . . . ' Her voice died away under a pair of clear, dark eyes that seemed to be able to read her thoughts — nightmare thoughts in which he lay hurt . . . 'Where were you anyway?' she demanded, with an angry little gesture that betrayed the concern that had driven her out into the dark more clearly than any words. 'I called and called . . . '

'I was in the barn,' he said, more gently. 'Trying to get the weather forecast on the radio. Apparently the storm has blown itself out. A warm front is moving in from the west.' He opened the door, then turned back. 'If you still want to do something, Abbie, you could make me a very large drink. You'll find some brandy in the cupboard.'

Her hands were shaking as she broke the seal on the bottle and poured a generous measure into a glass. It wasn't long before he returned, crossing quickly to the scullery to wash his hands. When he returned, he took the glass she offered, covering her hands with his cold fingers to steady her.

'You should have one too, Abbie. You don't look so good.' He bent down and took another glass from the cupboard, poured a drop into it and pressed it into her hand.

'There's some quite good wine in there,' she said, over-brightly, trying not to show how his fingers wrapped about hers were sending dangerous messages racing through her body. She took a quick sip of the brandy, hoping it would steady her racketing pulse. 'Did Jon buy that too?' she asked. 'You never used to leave alcohol here.'

'He must have done. Although, looking at it, I think it probably came from his father's cellar.' He was sipping thoughtfully at the drink she had poured for him. 'It's not supermarket plonk. What with that, and a whole bottle of brandy, it suggests that he thought he might have to get the poor girl plastered. But your Polly doesn't sound like the unwilling victim of Jon's youthful lust.'

'She's not *my* Polly,' Abbie protested. 'She's her very *own* Polly.' She gave a little shrug. 'In fact I'm rather afraid that the brandy might have been her idea. She seems to think it should be dished out in tumblers for shock.'

'Does she?' His lips twitched into a smile. 'I wonder how many of her patients actually survive the treatment?'

She gave a little shrug to cover her own amusement. 'I think I was probably her first. Perhaps it's fortunate that I don't much care for brandy.'

'Treatment for shock, is it?' Grey continued to stare into his glass, apparently giving this piece of information considerable thought. Then he raised his eyes to hers. 'And . . . er . . . which of them do you suppose she thought would need it the most?' One dark brow kicked sharply upward in sardonic query.

Abbie gasped, caught herself in an attempt to stifle a wayward giggle. This was not a laughing matter. It was all terribly serious. But the giggle refused to be stifled. In fact the harder she tried to keep the corners of her mouth under control the worse it got, until without warning a bubble of soft, irresistible laughter burst into the quiet room.

She clapped a hand over her mouth

in an attempt to stem the tide, but it was too late. It was so long since she had laughed, really laughed, that it was as if the floodgates had been breached.

'D-don't!' she warned, as Grey turned away a second too late to hide the fact that his face too had creased in a broad grin. 'Oh, don't, Grey!' But it was too late. His shoulders were shaking, and a sudden guffaw of laughter ripped from his chest, filling the room.

'Shock!' He shouted with laughter. 'I'll give him shock when I get hold of him.' But the words were drowned in his laughter. 'I'm s-sorry. It's really not in the least bit f-funny,' he said, trying unsuccessfully to get a grip on himself.

She shook her head, quite unable to answer as she was shaken by another uncontrollable fit of giggles, and collapsed against his shoulder. It seemed the most natural thing in the world for him to gather her close, and they clung on to one another and finally gave up the struggle to stop laughing, allowing the sheer, tension-relieving bliss of it to sweep over them.

It was the tiny piping of the lambs that finally brought them crashing back to earth. 'Oh, look,' Abbie said, brushing the tears from her cheeks as the stronger of the two struggled up onto wobbly legs. 'Poor little things.' She lifted her head from Grey's shoulder to discover her face inches from his own, her mouth a second away from bliss.

'It's so long since I've laughed, Abbie, that I thought I had forgotten how,' he said, his voice ragged.

'Me too,' she murmured. She hadn't realised until that moment just how desperately unhappy she was. No wonder she had spilled out her heart to Polly's eager ears. And now she was in Grey's arms and his eyes tempted her; the sharp, clean outdoor scent of the wind that enveloped him tempted her.

Horrified at how easy it would be simply to surrender, she pulled back, disentangling herself self-consciously from his arms, and turned purposefully to the lambs. 'H-how are we going to feed them?' she asked quickly. 'Will they take cow's milk?'

There was a long, dangerous pause. Then Grey sank to his haunches and stretched out his hand to the lambs' eager nuzzling. 'I don't know. Hugh uses a special formula for orphan lambs.' He looked up. 'You know — like baby milk.'

She knew. 'Then we'll have to get them to the farm. If we carry one each inside our coats — '

He didn't argue, but said, 'It's too far for you to walk in this. I'll take them. You stay here.'

'And worry myself to death about you?'

His eyes gleamed darkly as he looked up at her. 'Why on earth would you do that, Abbie?'

'I — I'd worry about anyone out in this weather. It'll be much safer with two of us.' Anything would be safer than staying in the dangerous atmosphere of the cottage, where every word, every gesture reminded her so forcibly of the past, rekindling emotions and feelings best left buried.

'I don't think you should risk it,' he asserted, rising to his feet. 'You've been half-frozen once.'

'Well, you've a ready-made cure if I should succumb again,' she declared boldly. 'If you can bring yourself to apply it.' His face tightened so that every feature seemed to leap into focus, sharper, leaner. He had lost weight, she realised with dismay. 'I found that ewe, Grey,' she rushed on, shutting out the treacherous thoughts that tormented her. 'I'm not about to let her lambs die because I might get cold feet.'

'Even if they're going to end up as lamb chops on someone's plate?' he demanded harshly. Abbie stared down at the tiny creatures and one of them, the first-born, lifted its little head and bleated at her. She clapped her hand over her mouth as lunch came vividly back to haunt her.

'Oh, Polly,' she murmured as the

blood drained from her face. 'How could you?'

'What?'

'Buy lamb. She's going through a vegetarian phase. Or she was until yesterday . . . Her mother said it would wear off . . . '

He frowned. 'But if . . . Damn!' As she swayed on her feet he grabbed the brandy glass from the nearby table and thrust it to her lips. 'Just a sip. No more.'

She obeyed, because it was easier than fighting him, and she gasped as the spirit burned down her throat, spreading its warmth across her stomach. 'I'm sorry. A tendency to faint at the drop of a hat seems to be getting to be something of a habit.'

'Does it?' His arm was round her shoulders, grasping her tightly so that she had no choice but to face him. 'Why?' he demanded. 'What's the matter with you?' He seemed genuinely concerned.

'Nothing. Let me go,' she insisted,

keeping her eyes cast down. 'I'm fine.'

'You don't look fine. You've lost weight. Your cheeks are hollow . . . ' He caught himself. Then he very carefully put down the glass. 'How very stupid of me,' he said. 'I should have realised. It's what you wanted after all . . . '

'Wanted?'

'You're pregnant, aren't you?'

# 8

Pregnant. If only she were. If only she could have had his child . . . A part of him that no one could ever take away. That must have been what Emma had wanted. And now Emma had every-thing, while she was alone — would always be alone.

In that bleak moment Abbie wanted to hurt him, to bare her pain and let him see what he had done to her in depriving her for ever of the special fulfilment of motherhood, but as she raised lids heavy with the pain of her loss and met his eyes she saw with a shock that his expression was too intent, her answer was too important to him.

In that moment she knew that she was balancing on the edge of a bottomless chasm into which it would be all too easy to fall. A chasm into which some deep part of her wanted to fall. One touch, one look, would ignite a spark that might give her what she desired, but she would have to live with herself ever afterwards. She had made her decision. There was no way back. Last night had meant nothing . . . if it happened again . . .

'I . . . I thought you said I'd lost weight,' she said stupidly. She had to say something — break the tension that stretched the air between them somehow.

But he didn't back off. 'In the early weeks women sometimes lose weight.'

He knew that? Was he a 'new' man, who'd read all the books, studied natural childbirth? Oh, yes. Grey Lockwood had never done anything by halves. He would want to be involved in everything to do with his child. Anger snapped her back from the abyss, and the heady surge of adrenalin sent her heart pounding into overdrive, finally provoking her beyond the steely control that had kept her emotions under wraps for so long.

'Emma lost weight, did she?' Her flaring reaction startled him and that pleased her; it pleased her so much that she went on. 'Tell me, did you take her to the antenatal clinic every week? Natural childbirth classes?' He made a gesture that dismissed the idea as ridiculous, but she wasn't put off by that. 'How did you account for your time in your appointments diary, Grey? Was that covered neatly by the phrase 'case conference' too?' His head jerked back as if she had hit him.

'I should have told you,' he said. It was an appeal for her to understand, but she was beyond understanding.

'Too damn right you should!'

He shook his head. 'I should never have let Robert persuade me . . . Did it really matter that much to you?'

'Matter?' She stared at him. 'You were deceiving me . . . how do you think I felt? I sensed something was wrong. That you were hiding something from me. But never in my wildest nightmares . . . ' She couldn't go on.

'And Steve Morley offered you a sympathetic shoulder to cry on.' He was angry too now. 'Why didn't you come to me? You didn't even give me a chance to explain.'

'Because I didn't — ' She stopped herself just in time. She had been through six months of hell to give him something important. The chance to begin again. If she blurted out the truth now, in a rush of anger, it would all have been for nothing. She drew back a little, managed a shrug, although she couldn't have said how. 'Because I didn't want to,' she said, concealing her anger now, under the painful mask of indifference. 'Steve offered something new.' True enough. He had offered, she just hadn't taken him up on it. 'Maybe I was just ready for that.'

'In a pig's eye! You were hurt and angry and he took advantage of that. Oh, God, what a mess! I'm sorry, Abbie.' He seized her hands. 'So sorry. It seemed the best thing to do at the time. I never meant to hurt you.

Hindsight is so clear — it's so easy to see now the way that secrets create an atmosphere that distorts everything, even love . . . '

She was rigid with shock as he poured out his remorse, unable to speak, unable even to take back her hands. Grey shook his head as if unable to go on. To see him hurting, to be unable to help him, was almost more than flesh and blood could stand. But she had to stand it. He had made his choice and he would have to live with it — as she did.

He gathered himself. 'You should look after yourself, Abbie. Rest — '

'Keep your antenatal advice for those who need it,' she told him, finally finding the strength to snatch back her hands from his warm grasp. 'I'm not expecting a baby — not that it would be any of your business if I were.'

For a moment she thought relief touched his eyes, but it was so fleeting, so unlikely that it actually mattered to him, that she dismissed it. 'We are still married, Abbie. Everything you do concerns me.'

'For a few more days. That's all.'

His head came up sharply. 'Have you signed the papers?'

'I only received them yesterday. They're in my bag. Out there in the snow.'

'You brought them with you in case you passed a convenient postbox? Were you in that much of a hurry to end our marriage?'

'I'm sure you couldn't wait to put your name to the papers,' she retaliated defensively.

'I've had other things on my mind.' He looked at her. 'Look, Abbie, just in case . . . if there's any possibility that you might be pregnant . . . you shouldn't be around pregnant sheep.'

'Well, there isn't and I'm not,' she snapped. Never have been and never likely to be, she thought bitterly. *Unless* . . . The word popped unbidden into her head and her eyes flickered back to Grey. Unless last night produced some kind of miracle. The timing was right . . .

She caught her breath and his eyes narrowed. 'What is it?'

She shook her head. 'Nothing.' The second lamb lying nearest her butted at her leg, then struggled to its feet and with a tiny wavering bleat demanded to be fed. She reached down, touched its head. 'Not lamb chops,' she promised it. 'Not if I have to rent a field and keep you for the next ten years.' And when she glanced up, she surprised such a look of tenderness on Grey's face that she smiled. 'Come on,' she said. 'We'd better get going. This little chap's hungry.'

His mouth straightened in a wry smile. 'If you're seriously planning to keep livestock, Abbie, you've one or two things to learn. Your little chap is a ewe. They both are.'

The blizzard had blown itself out. The evening sky was brilliant with stars and, once out of the sheltered hollow where the cottage lay, the snow was not so deep. It crunched and squeaked beneath their feet as they made their way up the narrow path towards the farm that nestled on the far side of the hill.

'All right?' Grey's hand shot out and caught Abbie's arm to steady her as she slipped a little on the frosted snow.

'Fine. I'm fine,' she said breathlessly, pulling free of his supporting grasp and stopping to stamp the snow out of the tread of her boots. Any excuse to rest for a moment, because she wasn't feeling fine at all. She was horribly aware that despite the fact she was forcing her legs to go through the motions, Grey was reining in his stride to match hers. The still, sharp cold bit painfully at her cheeks, fingers and toes, and as she dragged air into her lungs it hurt.

'We're nearly there,' he said encouragingly.

'Don't baby me, Grey,' she gasped. 'I know exactly how far we have to go.'

'Then be quiet and save your breath.'

And before she could protest, or stop him, he had removed the scarf from about his neck and had wrapped it around her face, covering her nose and mouth so that the sharp air was warmed before it hit her lungs.

'Grey, don't be silly . . . ' she mumbled, but he raised a warning finger, linking his arm firmly under hers, and somehow his strength seemed to transmit itself to her and she found a second wind, so that ten minutes later they breasted the hill, saw the lights of the farm beneath them, heard the anxious voices of the ewes in the lambing shed.

They paused for a moment to catch breath, and as they stood there the moon appeared from behind a scudding cloud, turning the sea below them to gleaming pewter, illuminating the glistening virgin snow.

'It should be Christmas,' Abbie whispered, and she looked down at the barn below them, heard the bleating of the sheep on the still air. 'There should be bells.'

Grey turned to her. 'And if it was,' he asked, 'what present would you want to find under your Christmas tree?'

She gave a quick shrug, but whether he saw it under her heavy layers of clothing she couldn't tell. She knew what she wanted most in the entire world, but that was her own deep secret. 'Come on,' she said. 'Let's go.'

Hugh looked up as they appeared in the doorway. 'Well, well,' he said, with a nod. 'Nice night for a walk if you've nothing better to do.' His weather-hardened face split into a broad grin at his own dry wit.

'We've brought you a couple of orphans,' Grey said. 'I'm afraid the ewe didn't make it.'

'Well, well,' Hugh said again, and straightened. 'I went out with the dog looking for her, but the weather was so bad we had to turn back.' His glance fell on Abbie, pinched and white with the cold. 'Better take them indoors, *bach*. Nancy will look after them.'

'You're on your own?' Grey asked,

looking around. 'I'll come back and give you a hand if you like.'

Nancy handed Grey a flask of tea to take back out with him and then turned to the lambs. 'I'm not sure which of you looks the worse for wear, Abbie, you or these little ones,' she said.

'I'm fine.' But as she held her hands out to the fire her teeth began to chatter audibly. 'J-just a b-bit cold.' She tried a reassuring smile but her mouth, juddering idiotically, refused to co-operate.

'A *bit* cold, is it?' she scolded cheerfully. 'Your jeans are soaking wet and you're shivering like a sick child. Straight upstairs with you and into the bath. I'll find you something warm now to put on.'

'But the lambs,' Abbie protested. 'Shouldn't we be doing something for them?'

'Not you, *bach*, me. And indeed the sooner you do as you're told, the sooner they'll be seen to,' she said. 'Upstairs with you now.' The farmhouse only had two bedrooms, the third little boxroom

231

having been converted to a bathroom by Hugh's father years before. 'Out of those wet things now, there's a bathrobe behind the door.'

And, assuming total obedience, Nancy bustled off to the airing cupboard to fetch fresh towels. She reappeared a few minutes later with a nightdress and a thick dressing gown and thrust them at Abbie. 'You might as well put these on,' she said, picking up the damp clothes that Abbie had discarded. 'You won't be going out again tonight. Supper will be ready when you come down.'

'But, Nancy — ' she began. There was no way that they could stay the night.

'I don't suppose they're quite what you're used to,' the older woman said with a laugh as she retreated in the direction of the kitchen, taking Abbie's wet clothes with her. 'But they're warm.'

'Thanks,' she called, somewhat belatedly, as she looked helplessly at the garments. It would be wonderful to feel warm.

The bath brought a glow back to her cheeks, and feeling decidedly more human she dressed in the soft flannel nightdress that buttoned up to the neck with a frill. Nancy was right, she hadn't had anything like it since she was about ten. The dressing gown had the same comforting nursery feel — thick and fleecy in a cheerful red. It was supposed to reach the floor, but Abbie was a head taller than Nancy and, like the nightdress, it stopped just below her knees, looking decidedly odd. She tied it about her, and, in the absence of a comb, raked her fingers through her hair a couple of times and went downstairs.

Hugh and Grey looked up from the table as she entered the kitchen, feeling somewhat self-conscious in her unconventional attire. 'There now, *bach*, you look better than you did half an hour ago,' Hugh said, evidently very pleased with life. 'Have some *cawl* and Nancy's good bread, and you'll be fit for anything.'

Grey was regarding her appearance

with considerable amusement, a fact that she discovered irritated her. Ignoring him, she turned to Nancy. 'How are the lambs?' she asked.

'They're sucking well enough. I've tucked them up by the Aga. If they make it through the night, they'll probably survive.'

'Until they go to market,' Grey reminded her provokingly.

Abbie glared at him. 'If they survive, Hugh,' she said, 'I'd like to buy them.'

Hugh merely patted her hand reassuringly. 'Grey is teasing you, *cariad*. Since they're ewes I'll be keeping them in the flock.'

'Unless, of course, you have plans to take them back to London to keep as pets?' Grey said, refusing to leave it.

'And what on earth will you do with them in London?' Nancy demanded, with a laugh. 'Keep them in your lovely flat?' Nancy and Hugh had stayed with them once, when they'd come up for the Smithfield Show. 'You leave them here, Abbie,' she advised. 'They'll be a lot happier in the fields.'

But Abbie was tired of being teased. 'Perhaps Matthew would like them as pets,' she said, picking up her spoon and dipping it into the steaming meat and vegetable broth. For a moment an awkward silence descended on the table. Then Hugh turned to Grey to ask after his brother and Nancy began to chatter about the weather and the moment passed.

But it was not forgotten. When Nancy had borne the plates away to the scullery, refusing any help, and Hugh had gone off to look for a drop of something warming left over from Christmas, Grey turned on her. 'Why on earth did you have to bring up Matthew? Nancy's been kindness itself, but she hardly approves. There's no need to flaunt the situation.'

'Me?' He had brought his lover to the cottage with their child and he accused *her* of flaunting the situation?

He caught at her wrist as Hugh returned. 'And since they don't know that we've split up, I'd rather you kept it that way,' he hissed. 'You've embarrassed them enough for one evening.'

Didn't know? What on earth did they think had been going on, for heaven's sake? But she was prevented from demanding to know exactly what the neighbours thought of his indiscretions by the return of Hugh, holding an unopened bottle of single malt that looked suspiciously like the one they had given him the Christmas before last.

Grey was right about one thing: Nancy was strict chapel, and as Hugh caught his wife's disapproving eye he said, 'Why don't you come through to the parlour, Grey. Leave the women to their gossip.'

'Shouldn't we go back out to the shed?'

'Nothing doing for half an hour or so. Might as well put our feet up by the fire.'

Grey hesitated, apparently unwilling to leave her to gossip with Nancy. 'Well, now, here we are.' Nancy bustled back with a tray. 'I made a few Welsh cakes yesterday. We'll have them with a cup of tea, Abbie, while you tell me all about your travels. I read your piece about that poor woman who had her little girl snatched. Terrible thing. Did she ever get her back?'

Abbie turned away from Grey's insistent gaze. 'Yes, she did eventually. She spent months in the mountains, travelling from village to village. She had a terrible time, but I think her dogged refusal to give up finally won her a kind of respect. To see someone endure so much for pure love touches the heart . . . ' The door clicked shut behind her.

'Well, well,' Nancy said. 'You must be very pleased. You're away such a lot these days, but if what you do helps . . . '

Nancy was easy to talk to, she did most of the work. She rattled on about what had been happening in the village, about the farm, and all Abbie had to do was drop in the occasional word to prompt her onto the next saga. Then a yawn caught her by surprise and Nancy tutted.

'There's me rattling on about nothing when you should be in bed. Come along, now, I've put in a bottle to air the bed.'

'No, really, Nancy, we can't put you to all this trouble.'

Nancy put her hands on her hips in a stance that brooked no argument. 'It wasn't any trouble coming all this way in the snow with two lambs, I suppose?'

'But I don't think we locked the cottage door . . . ' she protested.

'And who do you think is going to tour the neighbourhood in this weather, trying doors on the off chance that there's something worth stealing?'

Nancy was right, the whole idea was ridiculous. But she didn't want to go upstairs and lie in that big double bed waiting for Grey to come in. 'Then can I help with the lambs? They'll need feeding through the night and you've got enough to do.'

'Don't you bother your head about it. You've done enough.'

But Abbie had a stubborn streak too. 'I can take a turn, at least. I won't go to bed unless you promise to wake me.' She glanced at her watch, and saw to her chagrin that it was only nine-thirty. 'Call me at twelve. Promise?'

Nancy gave her a little push in the direction of the stairs. 'All right,' she said. 'I promise.'

\* \* \*

She woke with a start in a strange room and a strange bed, and for a moment panic swept over her. Then she remembered. She groped for the bedside light and peered at her watch. It was past one o'clock and Nancy hadn't called her. She swung her feet out of bed but as they hit the rug she saw Grey, slumped in the chair in the corner. For just a second she thought he was asleep and she froze, unwilling to risk waking him.

'There's no need to get up, Abbie.'

His voice rumbling from the dim recesses of the room startled her and she sank back onto the bed. 'Didn't the lambs survive?'

'They're going to be fine. One of the other ewes lost her lamb and Hugh convinced her that our orphans were hers.'

'How — ?' Then she shuddered as she remembered. 'No, don't tell me.'

'I didn't intend to.'

The farmhouse did not have central heating, and her breath smoked out towards him in the cold air. 'Why are you sitting there?' she asked, shivering.

'It's called keeping up appearances, Abbie. I would have stayed out in the lambing shed, but Hugh caught me yawning and turned me out. And since he and Nancy don't actually seem to go to bed at all during the lambing season, I had no choice but to come up here.'

She slipped on the thick robe and crossed to him. 'You must be freezing.'

She stretched out her fingers to his hand, but he pulled back. 'You can't sit there all night.'

'I'll be fine, Abbie. Go back to bed.'

She saw how he was huddled into the chair and knew that he wasn't fine. He was far from fine. He had been out in the lambing sheds for hours and she had no idea how long he had been sitting there. Her own concern about sharing the bed with him seemed petty in the extreme. 'For heaven's sake, Grey, we can be adult about this, surely?'

'Adult?' His voice mocked the word. 'Why, Abbie, whatever do you mean?'

'You know what I mean,' she said crossly. 'We can surely share a bed without . . . well, without . . .'

He rescued her. 'You've changed your tune since this morning.'

'This morning you weren't half frozen to death. Come to bed.'

'I can't, Abbie.'

She knelt in front of him, took his cold hands in hers and pressed them against her cheek to warm them. 'Then I'll have to sit up with you.'

'Please! Please, don't do this!'

She looked up at him, shocked by the pain in his voice. 'What is it?'

His eyes glittered in the lamplight as their breath condensed and mingled. 'I can't get into bed with you, Abbie. Just leave it at that.'

'This is silly. I'll stuff a bolster between us if that'll make you happy — '

'No!' he shouted. Until that moment she hadn't realised they had been whispering. 'You don't understand,' he said, his voice lower, but still insistent.

'Then you'd better do your best to make me understand, Grey,' she replied, with equal vehemence, 'because I'm staying here until you do.'

'Abbie!' He pleaded with her, but she took no notice of him, curling up against his leg, laying her cheek along his hard, denim-clad thigh. He touched her sleek, dark blonde head. 'Abbie, look at me.' She lifted her face to his and he cradled it between his hands, so that her warm cheeks lay against his freezing fingers. That must be why she was shivering despite the thick dressing gown.

'While I stay here I can continue to pretend that last night was the result of the cold. If I get into bed with you I'm going to have to admit that I've been lying to myself.' She tried to interrupt but he laid a finger over her lips. 'I'm going to have to admit that last night had nothing to do with hypothermia or first aid or even plain, unadorned lust. It had everything to do with desire. I'm going to have to admit to myself that I was capable of desiring you to the point where it blotted out everything else. And if I lied to myself, I lied to you.'

His fingers slipped from her face and he slumped back in the chair. 'So, if it's all the same to you, I'd rather sit here in the cold and keep my self-respect.'

This morning she'd thought she wanted to hear that. She'd thought she'd give anything to wake in his arms and hear him say those words. But now she knew that she had been wrong. To believe he loved someone else was a nightmare. If she allowed herself to believe that he loved her, allowed herself to hold him and tell him that she had wanted it too, it would destroy them both. What she had to do now, in this freezing cold room, was make him hate her enough not to care.

'Well, that's very noble of you,' she said, rising to her feet, turning away. She shrugged out of the dressing gown and with what she hoped sounded like careless indifference said, 'I'm sure Steve will find it highly amusing when I tell him that you still want me so much that you'd rather freeze to death than risk getting into bed with me.' She lifted the covers and eased herself back into bed.

'When you what?' He was on his feet and across the room in a stride. 'You're going to run back to your lover and tell him — '

It was working, but she had to be careful not to overplay her hand. 'You didn't think I'd keep it a secret from him? That's *your* way of handling unpalatable truths. But I don't believe in keeping secrets, Grey. Not from someone you're supposed to love.'

'Well, we might as well give him something to have a real laugh about,' he declared, angry enough to kill.

He pulled his shirt and sweater over his head, not bothering to turn away as he stripped off his remaining clothes and tugged back the covers. She rocketed across to the cold part of the bed, but the mattress sagged, and as he hit the mattress his weight brought her crashing back against his body and his arm shot out and pinned her there.

'Now,' he said grimly, 'what do you think would most *amuse* Mr Morley?' His eyes were inches from hers, gold lights sparking angrily in the warm autumn depths. 'It's been a while, but I'm sure I can remember — '

'I'm sure you can, Grey,' she said quickly, shaking from the impact of his aroused body so close. She swallowed.

She hadn't expected quite such a dangerously instant reaction to her taunts. 'But I know you'll understand if I tell you that I've . . . um . . . got a headache.'

'A headache?' For a moment he held her crushed hard against his ribcage, and there was no indication that he had any intention of understanding. For a moment everything was silent, the air taut as elastic, until, with a slow, deliberate expulsion of breath, he reached out and switched off the bedside light.

Abbie held her breath, still fastened by his hard, sinewy arm against his chest, very much afraid that she had misjudged him, driven him beyond the point of no return. Then he turned back to her.

'Turn round, Abbie,' he said, and she obeyed instantly, seizing her freedom as he moved his arm, but congratulating herself too soon as he scooped her flannel-wrapped body back against him. 'It's all right,' he murmured as she stiffened, his sweet breath on her cheek as his lips brushed her hair. 'You're perfectly safe. But I wouldn't try that trick with anyone who doesn't know you as well as I do. They might not understand. Go to sleep, now. We'll talk about it in the morning.'

Sleep? With his body curved about her? With her back against his chest, her hips pressed into his groin? She was just grateful for the thick flannelette night-dress, which muffled the urgent peaking of her breasts in its deep folds, as his arm, draped protectively over her, provoked a yearning ache for him deep within her.

* * *

Abbie woke, and turned in the warm bed to discover that she was alone. She was always alone. She ached for a different time, when Grey would have been there, when he would have reached for her in that early-morning quiet.

Yesterday she had been angry with him for leaving her to go and sleep in a chair. But it hadn't been that simple. His desire for her had driven him away, and she understood that now. Even in her fitful sleep she had been painfully conscious of him lying alongside her all the long night, and she understood why he hadn't waited for her to wake up. To wake against a warm, enticing body was to be utterly defenceless — at the mercy of the moment. He knew that as well as she did — he was fighting it too.

She rose, washed and scrambled into yesterday's clothes — dried and left on the chair for her — then walked, with an odd reluctance to face the day, to face him, down the stairs.

In the doorway she stopped. Unaware of her presence, and singing softly to himself, Grey turned bacon in the pan. The kettle began to boil and he lifted it from the hob, pouring water onto the tea. His movements were so spare, so effortless. He was a man who fitted his environment. In the City he wore a suit, commanded instant respect from his peers, stood head and shoulders above the crowd.

In the country he looked as if he had never seen a City desk.

There was a tray on the table, laid for one. He was going to bring her breakfast in bed. He had only ever done that when she was ill, or when he'd wanted to say that he was sorry. Rare enough. The small choking noise in her throat must have reached him over the sound of his own voice orchestrating some appallingly cheerful overture. He stopped, turned and smiled. Oh, God, he smiled. Not one of those tight, restrained smiles which had punctuated the past twenty-four hours, but the kind of smile that came straight from the heart.

But she couldn't allow herself the luxury of smiling back. His body against hers was too recent, too bittersweet an experience. She had to keep her distance, pretend that it had never happened. So she didn't smile. Although it broke her heart, she didn't smile. Instead she forced a brightness into her voice. 'You should have woken me,' she said.

Grey's smile faded. 'I shook you for half an hour. You didn't stir, so I thought I'd better bring you up a tray.'

'Liar,' she said, fielding the joke with a carelessness that hurt.

'Well, perhaps twenty minutes.'

'That's more like it. How are the lambs?'

'They're fine.'

'Really? You wouldn't just say that . . . '

'I'm not about to lie over the fate of a couple of lambs.' Why? Weren't they important enough to lie about? Unaware of the fury he had provoked in her breast, he lifted the bacon onto a plate and cracked a couple of eggs into the pan. 'Since you're up, you might as well make yourself useful and get on with the toast.'

She had no intention of making herself useful. She certainly didn't want any breakfast. 'Where's Nancy?' she asked.

'She's still in the milking parlour. She and Hugh had breakfast some time ago.'

'I'll take them out some tea and I can

say goodbye at the same time,' she said.

He looked up. 'They'll have tea when they come in. And you're not going anywhere until you've had something to eat.' She opened her mouth to protest. 'I mean it, Abbie, so don't even bother to argue.' She didn't. She recognised the look and closed her mouth, picked up the bread-knife and hacked a couple of pieces off the loaf before dumping them in the toaster. Apparently satisfied with this demonstration of obedience, he turned back to the pan. 'Abbie, about last night . . . ' he began.

'Forget it.'

He swivelled back to her. 'You keep telling me to forget things. Good things. Why?'

'Because . . . ' She trailed off. Challenged, she was unable to offer an answer. She picked up the teapot and began to pour out two huge mugs of the stuff so that she wouldn't have to meet his eyes. 'I couldn't leave you sitting in the cold,' she said stiffly. 'I mean . . . I wouldn't have the first idea how to go about dealing with a *genuine* case of hypothermia.'

'Ah.' He turned to face her. 'You're sore that I lied about that.' He regarded her steadily. 'Then I suppose, after last night, you could say honour is about even. I mean, you're not about to rush back to Steve Morley and tell him your midnight secrets, are you, Abbie?'

'Honour?' She grasped at the word in order to evade answering him. 'You have the nerve to use that word?'

He wasn't fooled. 'You're avoiding my question. Are you and Morley still together?' He didn't wait for her reply. 'I warn you, don't lie to me, Abbie, because I'll find out.'

'It's none of your business.'

He deftly slipped the eggs onto the plates and looked up at her. 'I'm making it my business,' he informed her. 'And, unwittingly or not, you've already answered my question. Is the toast ready yet?'

It burst from the toaster, making her jump. She turned quickly to butter it, keep her hands busy. Her head wasn't so easily distracted. It was all going wrong. Stupidly wrong.

She just couldn't understand why he was determined to find out what she was doing. It didn't matter what she was doing or who she was doing it with. At least, it shouldn't matter. She flickered a glance in his direction. But somehow it did.

# 9

Grey put a plate in front of her. She stared at the food. Perfectly plain, good food. After a moment he said, 'You might as well eat it hot, Abbie. Because you're going to eat it before you leave here. One way or another.'

She shook her head. 'I was just thinking about Polly.' Anything was better than thinking about the mess she and Grey had made of their lives.

He was unimpressed. 'You can eat and think at the same time.'

'Did I tell you that she was going through a vegetarian phase?'

'I think you mentioned it. Why?'

'I cooked some bacon one day and she left the room. She couldn't bear to watch me eat it, she said. She kept seeing little pink piglets . . .'

'It's quite common, you know, for young girls to go through that sort of thing — '

'You don't understand,' she interrupted, a little impatiently.

'If you're trying to make a specific point, Abbie, then you'll have to try harder.'

'It was on Sunday. The day before she and Jon took off.' She shook her head. 'It might just be a phase she's going through, Grey, but somehow I just can't believe she would change back into a ravening carnivore overnight. There was *nothing* at the cottage for her . . .'

He stared into the mug of tea. 'But if Jon did the shopping?'

'You're not suggesting he didn't know? She'd been trying to convert him for weeks . . . Besides, Polly has a somewhat managing disposition — I'm sure she would have given him a list. Even at seventeen she's perfectly well aware that no man is to be trusted alone in a supermarket.'

For a moment he regarded the bacon on her plate before raising his eyes to hers. 'Tell me, Abbie,' he said at last, 'just how difficult did little Polly

Flinders make it for you to work out where she had gone?'

'Difficult?' She gave a little shrug. 'It wasn't difficult at all. I mean, you telephoned and practically told me . . . Did Jon know you were thinking of taking him to Wales?'

'I mentioned it.'

'So he'd know you would look for the keys?' She lifted her head and met his eyes head on. 'And, just in case, Polly telephoned Robert's housekeeper pretending to be a journalist.'

'Why didn't she phone me?'

'Because you would have seen through her. I think the answer to your question, Grey, is that she and Jon didn't make it very difficult at all. In fact they laid a trail.' Abbie raised her hands to her face and, elbows on the table, propped her head on her hands. 'Oh, good grief, I can't believe that I've been so slow-witted. Lying in the snow must have frozen my brain.'

'But why? Why have they lured us down here, supplied us with a selection

of our favourite food and disappeared?'
He swore. 'They've backtracked. While
they've been jerking our strings, strand-
ing us here, they could be anywhere.
They knew we wouldn't just wait for
them to come back on Monday. That
we'd come after them — '

'They couldn't know that we'd be
snowbound, Grey,' she pointed out.

He considered this, a frown furrow-
ing his brow. 'Then what on earth are
they up to?'

Abbie was very afraid that she knew
what they were up to, but admitting it
wasn't going to be easy. She took a
deep breath. 'I think I'd better tell you
some more about Polly.'

'She's bright, pretty, clever and
managing. Are you telling me there's
more?' he demanded.

'Would you like some more toast?'
she asked, slicing into the loaf. He
made an impatient gesture which she
took as an affirmative. 'Tea?'

'Abbie!'

She looked up. 'Promise not to be

angry with them. They clearly didn't understand what they were doing.'

'I'm promising nothing,' he thundered. She picked up her knife and fork and began to eat. For a moment he watched her and fumed. Then he reached across the table and caught her wrist. 'I promise,' he said impatiently. She lifted her eyes, her glance challenging him. 'I promise,' he repeated, more gently this time. 'Obviously they're somewhere safe, or you would be bouncing off the ceiling by now.'

'I haven't the faintest idea where they are. Unless . . . ' She gave a little gasp, raising her hand to her mouth. 'Oh, no, they wouldn't be that cheeky.'

'Since this has been a very one-sided conversation, I haven't any idea. But, taking the situation so far, I wouldn't count on it. Now, are you going to let me in on the joke?' he demanded.

'It's not funny.'

'Then why are you grinning like a Cheshire cat?'

'I'm sorry.' She rapidly straightened

her face and, pushing her plate to one side, she tried to think how on earth she was going to explain what Jon and Polly were up to without betraying herself. 'The trouble is that Polly is a romantic.'

'I think I've grasped that already. But she's seventeen. At that age it's to be expected.'

'Perhaps. But I'm afraid she took it into her head that I was . . . ' there was no easy way to say it ' . . . well, that I was still in love with you.' She stared at a knot in the table, waiting for the exclamation of disgust. There was nothing but the sudden collapse of fuel in the grate to make her jump.

'Why would she think that, Abbie?' His voice was deceptively gentle. She had heard that tone before, leading people on until they were deep in some quagmire from which it was impossible to extricate themselves.

'Oh, that was your fault,' she declared brightly.

'*My* fault?' The words had a dangerous edge to them.

259

'Well, yes. It was the photograph album. It wasn't on your beautifully efficient list, you see. Polly opened the carton and there it was right on top. Being young and thoughtless, she opened it. It was a bit of shock . . . ' Like a kick in the stomach from a mule. She was still bruised.

'The kind of shock you needed a tumbler full of brandy for?'

She sidestepped the shock, concentrated on the brandy. 'Enough to put me under the table for a week if I'd drunk it all,' she said, with a wry little lift of her lips. 'When she realised who you were, that you were Jon's uncle, she just went on and on. There were some pictures of the cottage and she wanted to know all about that too.'

'Why didn't she ask Jon? He's been there often enough.'

'Oh, I'm sure she did. In fact, on reflection, I think he must have been priming her,' she said thoughtfully. 'She once asked me what a slurry pit was.' She raised her eyes to Grey's.

'So you told her all about the time one of Hugh's cows knocked me into one, I suppose. I've no doubt the two of you howled with laughter.'

'I'm afraid so.' She bit her lower lip, trying not to laugh now. It had been dangerous, horribly dangerous.

'If you'd been on the other end of the hosepipe, you wouldn't have thought it was so funny, I can tell you.' She shook her head, unable to speak. 'Damn it, you had to break the ice off the damned thing before you could even unravel it.'

'If I'd let you into the cottage we would never have got rid of the smell,' she gasped.

'And as if it wasn't bad enough being stripped to the buff while you hosed me down with ice water . . . ' a bubble of laughter finally escaped Abbie's lips ' . . . some wretched woman chose that moment to come into the yard shaking her collecting box for suffering animals.'

'It wasn't *personal*, Grey,' she gasped. 'The cow didn't mean you any harm, and the poor woman didn't come *very* close. The smell . . . '

Grey finally succumbed to a grin. 'No, well, she could see I didn't have any pockets for loose change. I always promised myself that one day I'd turn the hose on you . . . ' He walked to the far side of the room, as far away as he could go. For a moment — just for a moment — it had been as if nothing had changed. 'So,' he said abruptly. 'I think I've got the general idea. Polly thought if we were stranded together overnight nature could be left to take its course.' He propped his elbow on the mantle. 'She's clever, I think you said. In the circumstances I'd have to agree.'

'I don't imagine she had your somewhat drastic cure for hypothermia in mind.'

'She seems to have overlooked Steve Morley as well. Or didn't you bother to fill her in on all the sordid details?'

She had hoped he would miss the gaping holes in her tale, but he was too quick for that. 'I didn't fill her in on *any* details. Do you think if I'd told her the real reason for our break-up she would have gone to all this trouble?'

'No. In fact I find it hard to believe that a seventeen-year-old would go to so much trouble without a great deal of encouragement. It seems far more likely that after trailing around a lot of dreary flats you decided that my nest was infinitely more comfortable. Was that why you went to see Morley before you came down here? To tell him it was over?'

'I certainly told him to get lost, but not quite in the way you mean,' she said. 'He wanted — '

But Grey cut her off, not interested in listening to her explanations. 'Once you realised that Polly and Jon were friends it must have seemed so simple to manipulate the pair of them.'

'And am I supposed to have manipulated a blizzard, a car accident and my near demise in the snow?' she demanded.

He shrugged. 'They were just good luck.' Her explosion of rage bounced off him. 'I imagine you thought once you had me here I would be a pushover.'

'Why on earth would I think that?' she demanded, then flushed deeply as she realised, as he must do, that he had indeed been a pushover. 'And whatever was Jon thinking of?' she went on quickly. 'He must know what the situation is.'

'When your wife walks out on you for another man, Abbie, you don't exactly bellow it from the hilltops. You certainly don't discuss the details with an eighteen-year-old boy.'

'I would have thought you were finding the details just a little difficult to keep secret!' Or could it be that he was doing just that? Maybe Emma hadn't moved in with him. Maybe he felt that discretion was vital until after the decree absolute was granted. She shrugged. 'Well, I don't suppose it matters. Did you say the weather was clearing today? Maybe I can get back to London — '

He shook his head. 'The sun is out now, but the snow froze solid last night, and according to the local radio the road is still blocked halfway to Carmarthen — so I'm afraid you're stuck with your plot for another day or two. And, since you clearly know where Polly and Jon are, you can cut out the concerned babysitter routine.' He glowered at her. 'Where exactly are they, by the way?'

'I can't be sure, but I think they've probably helped themselves to your flat.' She regarded him levelly. 'Jon took her there once before, on the pretext of showing her the Degas. The one you sold for a great deal of money to set up a trust fund for Matthew. Tell me, Grey, doesn't Jon know that the picture apparently hanging in its place is simply a very good copy? Or is he as devious as you? Did he take his own?'

He stared at her. 'The Degas is genuine. I'm not sure which of your questions that answers. Take your pick.'

'Steve told me about the sale, Grey. It was in the paper, for heaven's sake. And it might have slipped your memory, but you told me yourself that you sold it to help Robert out of some financial difficulty — '

'I did.'

'And now you have it back?'

'Robert's difficulty was not a lack of funds, it was simply moving them without attracting attention — ' He stopped abruptly as the door behind her opened. 'Ah, Nancy, we were just saying that we should be getting back to the cottage. The fire will have gone out and everything will be freezing.'

'Have you had enough to eat — ?'

'Yes, thank you,' Abbie broke in, standing up. 'I'll just clear up. Can I make you a fresh pot of tea?'

'No. Not just now. And leave the dishes, *bach*.' She lowered herself heavily into a seat in front of the fire.

'It's no trouble,' Abbie said.

But Grey reached for her coat and began to feed her arms into the sleeves. 'Time to go. We don't want to outstay our welcome.'

'You'll never do that, Grey,' Nancy

said, with a laugh, but Abbie could see that she was already half asleep.

They grabbed their boots and put them on in the porch. 'She just wanted to doze off for an hour. I told you, they don't seem to go to bed during the lambing season, but if we'd stayed she'd have felt obliged to keep awake.'

They looked in on Hugh on the way out of the yard and Abbie saw that her lambs had truly settled with their foster mother. Then they set off back to the cottage.

The walk was less daunting in the daylight, and with the sun sparkling on the snow, and the sea reflecting the pale blue of the winter sky in the distance, it seemed picture-postcard perfect. The curl of smoke drifting straight up from the cottage chimney in the still air seemed to bring a final touch to the glistening landscape. A promise of warmth. Abbie stopped suddenly and Grey turned to her.

'What's the matter?'

'There's someone in the cottage,' she

said. 'The fire's lit. It can't possibly still be burning from last night.'

'Jon and Polly?'

They exchanged a look and broke into a slithering run. Grey was first through the door, shedding snow from his boots over the floor, and Abbie was close on his heels. They both came to an abrupt halt as the man bending over, prodding at the fire, looked up and smiled.

'Well, well, well,' he said, straightening. 'Mr and Mrs Lockwood, together again. How very charming.'

'What the hell — ?'

'Steve?' Abbie could hardly believe her eyes. 'How on earth did you get here? Are the roads open?'

'I'm afraid not. I came down on Monday afternoon, my dear, not long after our somewhat heated discussion. I had a report from the man who was tailing him that young Master Jonathan Lockwood came here over the weekend and stocked the place up with groceries before beating it back to London. I knew it wouldn't be long before someone more interesting came along and I was right. Unfortunately the snow kept me in the village until this morning.'

He turned back to the fire and threw on another log. 'You really shouldn't go out and leave the place unlocked, you know. Anybody might come in and help themselves to your brandy. Or is it your brother's?' He picked up a glass and tipped it back. 'He has excellent taste.'

'I'm glad it meets with your approval. Now you are most welcome to leave and to take my wife with you. Presumably that is why you're here?'

Before Abbie could utter a word Steve Morley smiled. 'Sorry, old man. Quick thinking, I grant you. But you've blown it. Not that I ever really believed in this little broken-hearted charade of yours, Abbie.'

'Charade?' Abbie looked from Steve's self-satisfied face to Grey's angry mask and felt like slapping them both. 'What are you talking about?'

'It's all right, my dear, no need to keep up the pretence. I don't blame *you*. Your husband would do anything for his brother and you would do anything for him. In a perfect world, that's how it should be.'

'But — ' she began, but Grey's fingers fastened around her wrist warningly.

'I doubt if I would have fallen for it in the first place if you hadn't seemed so genuinely shocked when I told you I had seen your loving husband lunching with a beautiful young woman.'

Abbie knew he was going to say something that would destroy everything, and she had to stop him. 'Steve — ' she said, taking half a step towards him, but Grey's hand held her fast.

'I think we should listen to the man, Abbie. Clearly he thinks he has a tale to tell. Since he's been kind enough to light the fire for us, why don't we take off our coats and join him in a glass of Robert's excellent brandy.'

Steve looked at Grey uncertainly. He knew what to expect when he was angry, but this calm, self-controlled mood clearly disturbed him far more. He shifted awkwardly as Grey finally released Abbie's wrist and helped her out of her coat.

'Fetch a couple of glasses, Abbie,' he said, with every appearance of good humour as he hung up their coats and stood their boots on the mat. Then he took the poker from an unresisting Steve Morley, riddled through the grate and made it up with the logs they had brought in the night before. 'Please, Mr Morley, do sit down and make yourself at home.'

It was extraordinary, Abbie thought, how a few seconds earlier Steve Morley had been in leering control of the situation, but, having too quickly accepted the invitation to make himself comfortable, he was now at a total disadvantage as Grey remained on his feet, leaning one elbow against the mantle, the poker swinging freely from his fingers. She handed Grey a glass an inch deep in the glowing amber spirit, and did not think twice about pouring another for herself. She was certain she was going to need it.

'So, Mr Morley. You saw me lunching with a beautiful young woman. I don't imagine that was just coincidence?'

'Hardly. Although I have to confess it was your brother I was expecting to see.'

'Then that answers my next question. Clearly it was Mrs Harper you were having followed, not me. So you thought you'd mention my little assignation to Abbie, hoping to pry loose some indiscretion . . . '

'Unfortunately it didn't work.' Abbie sank into the other chair as Steve replied, remembering the casual way that he had dropped it into the conversation that day at L'Escargot. Something about a 'pretty piece'. The man had an unbelievably vulgar turn of phrase. 'I mean, she'd been telling me that she wasn't going to take any more overseas jobs because she thought her marriage needed a little work, so I thought it was worth a chance. She was so shocked that I actually believed it . . . '

Abbie refused to look up, to face him, but she knew that Grey's eyes were on her. She could feel them burning into her brain. 'She's quite an actress, isn't she? I'm really very proud of her.'

*Actress!*

'You should be. When she told me that she had discovered her loving husband had been having an affair for months, that he had a child by another woman, well, I have to say that it isn't an award for photo-journalism she should have received, but an Academy Award.'

'Was she very convincing?'

'She convinced me.'

'Will you two stop talking about me as if I'm not here?'

Grey's hand rested lightly on her shoulder. 'Hush, love. Mr Morley has come a long way on a fool's errand, the least we can do is let him tell us just how big a fool he has been.'

'I'm not that much of a fool.' Steve regarded them both malevolently, all pretence of politeness wiped from his face. 'The minute you booked a seat on a flight to Atlanta I twigged. I mean, if my old lady had decided to walk away without any hassle, leaving me free and clear to get on with a new woman and a new baby, I sure as hell wouldn't have gone chasing after her.'

'Quite.'

'You should have seen your face. There you were, with your arms all wrapped nice and neat around each other, and I popped out of the bathroom.'

'It was quite an entrance.'

'Got carried away, did you, Abbie? Forgot I was there?' Steve shook his head. 'I have to admit that you put on the injured husband routine a treat, Mr Lockwood. I mean, I've seen the real thing and you still come top of the list.' He rubbed his jaw. 'I have the feeling you put everything you had into that punch you threw.'

Grey smiled slightly. 'If I convinced you, Mr Morley, the bruised knuckles were worth it.'

'But then there she was, weeping all over me, begging me not to put it in the papers.' Steve looked at Abbie. 'That's when she let you down, Mr Lockwood.'

Grey's fingers tightened on her shoulder. 'Let me down?'

'Well, there I was with a big broad shoulder, all ready to cry on, and under the circumstances you would have thought she would be grateful . . . '

'I'm afraid that there are some things that, even to protect my brother, I would not ask Abbie to bear.'

'Pity, that. Because when I got back from Atlanta I put the tail back on Mrs Harper. And guess what?'

'What?' Abbie was half out of her seat, the word uttered before her brain had engaged. She forced herself to relax back into the comfortable, baggy cushions. 'What happened then?'

'Well, to be sure Mr Grey Lockwood

frequently drove Mrs Emma Harper to some quiet country house. In fact I have hundreds of photographs of them arriving at all kinds of interesting places.' He paused as Abbie drew in a long, shuddering breath. 'Try a drop of that brandy, my dear, it's really very good.'

'I think you should get on, Mr Morley.' There was hardly any change to that urbane tone, yet Abbie knew that Grey was very near the edge of losing his temper. 'You're taking too long to come to your point.'

'Oh, right. Where was I?' He turned to Abbie. 'Oh, yes, your supposedly estranged husband arriving at some discreet retreat with Mrs Harper. His car staying there all night for the world to see.'

Her hand was trembling on the heavy glass and she put it down before she dropped it.

'It's quite striking — not the sort of car you would mistake ... But apparently only the car remained. I don't suppose I would ever have realised what was happening if I hadn't seen Mr Grey Lockwood, live on the ten o'clock news, discussing some benchmark case he'd won on behalf of his neighbourhood law centre, when his car was parked outside a house in St John's Wood.

'But he must have realised his mistake, because by the time I got to the house and rang the bell, with a photographer staking out every exit, well, there was Mr Grey Lockwood — a trifle short of breath, it's true, but wearing nothing more than a silk dressing gown — to open the door and invite us in for a nightcap. Since then Mrs Harper has been living quietly in a cottage on the river at Henley. And neither Mr Grey Lockwood or his brother have been near the house — not even in frogman's flippers.'

'That's all very illuminating, Mr Morley. What do you want me to say? That you've been a very clever boy?' Grey didn't wait for him to answer.

'Not quite clever enough, if you expected to find my brother *in flagrante* with Mrs Harper at Ty Bach.'

'Clever enough to have taken photographs of a cupboard full of baby equipment. Clever enough to have matched dates and times when *you* were supposed to be with Mrs Harper, but, oddly, your *brother* was also not available. And now I *know* that you two have been playing me for a fool — well, I have enough to make life extremely difficult for the Right Honourable Robert Lockwood, MP.'

'Why?' Abbie never had been able to understand why Steve Morley was so obsessed with hurting Robert.

'Why not? People like him set themselves above everyone else. It makes them a target.'

'No, they don't. Robert is a decent human being, trying to do a job.'

'He's a politician, with his sights set firmly on number ten. All holier than thou on the outside and cheating on his wife on the inside. And with you so close to the throne, so to speak, it was too good an opportunity to miss.' He drained his glass. 'You know, you were slow, Abbie. You should have taken the money I offered you to spill the beans. I mean, no one is as unselfish, as generous as you seemed to be. And a wronged woman would never have allowed her husband to get off scot-free. Human nature just isn't like that, is it?'

'Well, this has all been very illuminating, Mr Morley,' Grey said, moving towards the door. 'Don't let us keep you.'

Steve stood up a little uncertainly. 'Aren't you going to frisk me for the film?'

'Certainly not. That would be a gross infringement of your rights.'

'His rights!' Abbie exploded. 'What about our rights? He snooped, spied, took photographs . . . '

'He was only doing his job, Abbie. He didn't break in. The door was open. And you seem to forget that he very kindly lit the fire for us.'

'Oh, right . . . Perhaps we should invite him to stay for lunch?'

'There's no need to go that far. Besides, I'm sure he's absolutely dying to get to the nearest telephone. We shouldn't delay him.'

Steve Morley regarded Grey suspiciously. 'If you think the telephone lines being down will stop me, you're wrong. I have a portable telephone.'

'Of course you do. But I'm afraid it's not going to do you much good. Robert informed the Prime Minister that he would not be standing at the next election some time ago.'

'You think people won't still want to know — '

'But they do know. Or at least, they will. There will be a statement in the evening papers to the effect that he has resigned to spend more time with his family.' Steve Morley's snort of disgust made no impression upon Grey. 'His new family. Emma and Matthew. Jon, incidentally, is delighted with the arrangement. And I don't think the private life of an ex-politician will provide a great deal of news value. Not with the blizzard. And today's announcement that Mrs Susan Lockwood will be his party's candidate at the by-election.'

'What?' Steve Morley went white. He fumbled in his pocket for his portable telephone, but Grey plucked it from his hand before he could use it and removed the batteries, dropping them in his pocket before returning it to him.

'I'm afraid I really can't permit you to conduct your business under my roof. I'm fussy that way.' Grey glanced at his watch. 'But if you get a move on, you might catch the announcement on the one o'clock news.'

Steve did not need encouragement; he was already scrambling into his coat.

'It's such a pity,' Grey went on. 'You've been in the wrong place chasing the wrong story for the past couple of days, Mr Morley. You should have stayed in London; no doubt your paper's proprietor will want to know why you weren't at your desk.'

He took his coat from behind the door and stepped into his boots before opening the door. 'Now, I'll walk you down to the road. The lane can be treacherous in this weather, and I wouldn't want anything bad to happen to you.' He looked back at Abbie. 'I won't be long,' he said.

But as the door banged shut behind them she didn't find that promise particularly reassuring.

# 10

Abbie waited. For a long time she sat beside the fire and waited for him to come back, to tell her that he understood what she had done, why she had done it. She waited for him to say that everything was going to be all right. But he didn't come back.

When an hour had passed, she got up, cleared away the glasses, put the kettle on the range and searched the freezer for something to eat. They would still have to eat. Ordinary everyday things, to keep her mind occupied. To keep her thoughts from dwelling on the nightmare of what she had done.

Pan-fried steak, jacket potatoes, tomato salad. She ticked them off on her fingers as she laid out the ingredients, looked for peppercorns and, to her astonishment, found that even those had been thought of by Polly. She turned with the tub in her hand and he was there, his silent figure filling the doorway. The peppers rattled betrayingly against the plastic container.

'I didn't hear you come in,' she said. She hadn't been hearing anything except the silent scream of her heart . . . 'You were gone a long time. Wh-what did you do to Steve?'

'Does it matter?' He glanced at the food. 'If we're having steak, there's a claret to go with it. I'll open it now if you'll pass me the corkscrew.'

'Corkscrew?' Why were they talking about corkscrews?

'In the drawer behind you.'

'Did you hurt him?' she asked, head down, hunting through the muddle of the drawer. If he had lost his temper it would have been better than this cold indifference.

'Should I have done? He was just doing his job, no matter how distasteful. I would have thought having to justify the cost of pursuing Robert for the last twelve months and coming up empty-handed to a stony-faced newspaper proprietor would be far more sobering than anything I could dish out.' He had moved up behind her, and he looked over her shoulder and fished out the corkscrew from a tangle of string, taking great care not to touch her. 'Besides, he has a hard chin.' He flexed his hand, as if remembering the pain.

She turned against the sink unit to face him. 'I'm sorry, Grey. I should have trusted you . . . ' He shrugged and began to move away. 'Grey?' She put her hand on his sleeve. 'It was all a misunderstanding, don't you see?' His eyes remained blank of expression, cutting her off, freezing her out. 'Please, speak to me.'

'What do you want me to say, Abbie? I thought you were having an affair. You did go to some trouble to convince me of that, as I recall. You even managed to produce a naked man from your bathroom to prove the point.'

'I wanted you to be free — '

'Now I have to deal with the fact that

when this creep who spies on decent people for a living told you that he saw me having *lunch* with another woman you decided that I was cheating on you. Three years of respect and trust and love get dumped and I don't even get a chance to defend myself? Can you have any idea what that feels like?'

He removed her fingers from his arm, walked out of the scullery, leaned his forehead against the heavy beam over the fire and stared down into the flames. He was hurting. She could see that, understand that, but while he had been playing games to keep Robert's indiscretions out of the newspapers she had been hurt too.

'Is that what you really think, Grey?' she asked from the doorway. 'Do you really believe that I thought for one moment that you were being unfaithful to me just because of what Steve said? I admit it was a jolt, but then I thought, Oh, *come on*, Abbie. This is Grey we're talking about. He might have been a bit distracted lately, not exactly willing to listen when you asked him to discuss the rest of your life, but he's a straight-down-the-line kind of a guy. If he'd found someone else he would tell you. He would *never* deceive you . . . '

He turned his head to look at her. 'Then why?'

'Because I saw you. With my own two eyes. I dropped by your office to take you out to lunch and as I got out of the taxi I saw you walking down the road. You were too far away for me to shout, but I could see you were going into the park so I followed you. Not to spy on you, simply to catch up with you so that I could be with you.

'And do you know what I saw then?' His face drained of colour but she didn't spare him. 'I saw you put your arm around a beautiful woman and then bend over and touch . . . ' The words caught in her throat. 'I saw you touch her baby. So tenderly. So lovingly. You'd made it perfectly clear that you didn't want me to have your child and suddenly it all began to make sense — '

'No!' He straightened. 'Good grief, didn't I make it clear why I thought we should wait?'

'Matthew is the image of you when you were a baby.'

'He's the image of Robert too.' Then his eyes narrowed. 'How do you know what he looks like? Did you actually go across and look in his pram?'

'Women do that all the time. Look in prams, chat on park benches, tell total strangers all their problems. She never knew who I was.'

'You talked to Emma?'

'Yes, I talked to Emma.' It still hurt so much to remember that day. 'After you had gone I wanted to run away, pretend I hadn't seen anything. It was all so horrible.'

'But you couldn't?'

'Emma was so sweet, so open. And, considering her situation, very careless. I suppose she thought that she was safe because I was just another woman — a perfect stranger. Or maybe it was that she'd had to keep everything bottled up for too long and I just pushed the right buttons.' She gave a little shrug. 'Whatever. It all came pouring out. How her lover was a lawyer and a divorce would destroy his career — '

'Good grief, Abbie, divorced lawyers are ten a penny these days — like every other profession.'

'I know. And Robert is a lawyer too,' she said, with a little sigh. 'But it's so long since he practised that it never even occurred to me. All I could think of was poor Henry.'

'Henry? But that was different — he got involved with a client. He *caused* the divorce, for heaven's sake . . . ' His head went back. 'You thought that Emma had been my client?'

'There was a mark where she had worn a ring. It seemed . . . possible.'

'I sometimes forget that you're a journalist as well as a photographer, Abbie.'

'Not often enough, it seems. That's why you didn't tell me, isn't it? Did you think I'd put my career before my family?'

'No, of course not,' he said impatiently. Then he crossed to her, took her hands. 'I was simply trying to protect you, Abbie.'

His hands had been by the fire and were warm against her cold fingers. She looked up into his eyes. 'Protect me?' He'd said that before, and suddenly it made sense.

'From the likes of Steve Morley, who is just as good as you are at pressing the right buttons. And a great deal more ruthless about it.'

'I see.' And she did see. 'The trouble is, my love, that while you were busy convincing the rest of the world that it was *you* having an affair with Emma Harper, you convinced me as well.'

'It never crossed my mind that you would jump to conclusions and walk out without even giving me an opportunity to explain the situation. Besides, you were away so much — '

'That it didn't matter?'

'Of course it mattered,' he said bleakly. 'But you saw the lengths Steve

Morley was prepared to go to. If he'd thought you'd had any idea what was going on he wouldn't have given you a moment's peace. I suppose he told you about the trust fund for Matthew too?'

'No, he never mentioned it. He told me that he'd seen you, and that you'd sold the Degas, that was all.'

'Then how did you find out about it?'

'Even after I'd talked to Emma, seen Matthew, I tried to tell myself that it couldn't be true. That there had to be some explanation. But I had to know, Grey. So I came home and checked the credit card statements — and there it was, in black and white. All those trips to Wales when I was away. And for the day you told me you'd driven back from Manchester there was a voucher from a petrol station on the M4. It's odd, but I knew you weren't telling me the truth about that, but I couldn't think why. Lying is so alien to you that I just let it go.'

'It's the only direct lie I ever told you.'

'It must have been extremely inconvenient to have me arrive home unexpectedly. I don't suppose I'd have even known you'd been away but for that.' His silence answered her question. 'Indirect lies are just as bad, Grey,' she said.

'Yes, I suppose they are. I was trying to do the best I could for everyone.'

She pulled her hands away from his, shivered and walked across to the fire. She held out her hands to it, rubbed her arms. 'I saw the letter from the bank,' she said. 'Considering the circumstances, I thought it was rather careless of you to leave it lying around.'

'It was meant to be indiscreet. I'd had a copy leaked to Morley and I thought that would put an end to the matter until Robert could settle his affairs and leave the government without a scandal.'

'Well, lucky old Robert.'

'He only ever wanted to be a farmer, Abbie. But he knew that Dad expected him to follow him into the firm, and then Susan came along and she had much bigger plans for him. Robert was to be Prime Minister by the time he was fifty.'

'What about Susan? She's not really going to sit back and let Robert quietly resign from his post and then divorce her?'

'Well, yes, actually, she is. She comes from a family where the men do things and the women make the tea. She thought that was the way it had to be. But I convinced her that it isn't. She really is going to stand for his seat in the by-election. Politics was *her* ambition, Abbie. It was the frustration of seeing Robert do the things that she knew she could do as well — better, perhaps — that drove her crazy with jealousy. She's a changed woman.'

'I'm glad. Very glad it's all worked out so well for everyone.' She turned abruptly away from him. 'Now, if you'll excuse me, I have to get on with lunch.'

'Lunch can wait, Abbie.' His hands were on her shoulders and her shoulders were shaking. 'Oh, look, you're crying.' He turned her round to face him. 'You shouldn't be crying.' He pulled her rigid body close, so that her tears flooded onto his sweater. He tucked his fingers under her chin and lifted her face to his. It was serious, deadly serious. 'It's all over, Abbie. You know that, don't you?'

Over. She had thought it was over six months ago. She'd thought she had lost him, but she hadn't lost him — she had thrown him away. 'I didn't trust you enough. I've hurt you — ' She tried to pull free, but he wasn't letting her go. Instead he stroked away the tears from her cheeks with his fingers.

'Hurt?' he murmured softly. 'I didn't think it was possible to suffer so much and still live.'

'Do you think I don't know?' She knew that pain only too well, and she closed her eyes to blot out the agony of it. 'I'm sorry, Grey. I don't know what else to say.'

'Words won't do it, Abbie.' The tiny bud of hope that had begun to unfurl in her heart shrank back. 'Of course,' he continued, 'you could always try kissing me better.'

She lifted tear-jewelled lashes, saw the gold sparks heating the depths of his eyes. 'There's an awful lot of you to kiss, Grey. I — I really wouldn't know where to begin.'

'Then let me show you.' He dropped a kiss on the top of her head and it somehow fluttered down onto her forehead. 'You see? You start at the top and just . . . work down.'

His mouth brushed her temple, the high, blushing cheekbone, the delicate hollow beneath her jaw, and suddenly it was not a game any more, and as his lips lightly crossed hers the glorious weakness in her legs left her clinging to him. For a moment they were suspended there, lips a millimetre apart.

'I love you so much, Abbie,' Grey murmured huskily. 'So very much.' And then his lips were on hers, sweet, demanding, loving, telling her that the nightmare was over. After a long while he lifted his head. 'Do you think you've got the hang of it so far, my love?'

She was *his* love. His *love*. Was it possible that she could ever show him how much he was hers? Steadying herself with her hands on his shoulders, she stood up on her toes, determined to try. 'I can't reach the top,' she said.

'No?' His smile was teasing as he stood there, straight as a ramrod, making no attempt to help her by bending, even a little bit.

'I'm afraid . . . ' she began and he waited, not making any effort to ease her difficulty. 'I'm afraid that I'm going to have to ask you to lie down.'

He regarded her with the slow, teasing smile that seemed to go on and on for ever. 'Abbie?'

'What is it?'

'You will be gentle with me?'

Her own mouth straightened into the widest smile. 'Don't count on it, Grey Lockwood — ' But the threat disintegrated into a scream as he picked her up and carried her up the stairs.

* * *

'Abbie?' She turned sleepily in his arms and nestled against his shoulder. 'I love you. I don't know how to tell you how much I love you.'

She opened her eyes, wide awake now. 'You punched Steve Morley on the chin. That says it all. I should have known. I mean, if a louse like Steve could work it out, why couldn't I?'

'I still don't understand why you didn't say anything. Most women would have screamed, raged, smashed the china. Keeping you in the dark about what was really happening was bad enough . . . but what you thought was going on has driven less balanced women to murder.' He drew her closer into the curve of his arm. 'But then you always were cool under pressure.'

'Oh, not that cool. I wanted to hurt you, Grey. I was going to plaster your family in headlines a foot high across the tabloids. And then Susan rang and it was like hearing an echo of the words in my head. Horrible words. Hateful words.' Grey turned to her, held her comfortingly in his arms. 'I know that some of it was my fault, you see. I was never there. I was always away chasing the perfect story, the one that would make my name. And I thought you had found someone to fill the gap. A delicate, beautiful, *little* part-time wife.'

He swore softly. 'I didn't mean it, idiot. I love every inch of you.'

'Do you?'

'All seventy-one of them,' he assured her seriously.

'Seventy!' She flung a fist at his shoulder and he laughed. 'Rat,' she murmured, but, as he proceeded to kiss every inch to prove his point, it was a while before she could continue.

'I thought if I went away for good, made you think it didn't matter, you could get on with your new life. No complications, no guilt.'

'You really did that for me?' He rocked her gently. 'Oh, Abbie, sweetheart, is it any wonder that Steve

Morley didn't believe it? Self-sacrifice is the purest of all the emotions. I doubt he's ever encountered it before.'

★  ★  ★

Abbie was cooking breakfast when there was a sharp rap at the door. 'Come in,' she called, expecting to see Hugh. But it was the postman, who put his head around the door.

'Is this yours?' he asked, holding out her bag. 'I found it down the lane, sticking out of the snow.'

'Oh, yes. Thank you so much for bringing it all the way up here.'

'I had to come anyway. I've a letter for you. Sorry for the delay — it should have been here Tuesday, but the roads have only just opened up.' It was postmarked with Monday's date and addressed to Mr and Mrs Lockwood.

'How is it out there?' she asked, turning it over.

'Passable. Although I see someone ended up in the ditch.'

'Oh, that was me, I'm afraid. No damage done, except to the car. If you're going into the village can you get someone to tow it down to the garage for me?' The postman, quite used to unusual requests from the more isolated dwellings on his round, assured her that it would be done.

'What's that?'

Abbie looked up as Grey walked down the stairs. 'A letter. From Polly and Jon, I think.'

'Oh, Lord, the runaway lovers. I'd forgotten all about them. What do they have to say for themselves?'

She opened it and began to read. ''Dear Abbie and Grey (I hope you don't mind me calling you that, but Dear Abbie and Mr Lockwood sounded silly) . . . ''

Abbie looked up and met Grey's eyes. 'Do you mind?' she asked.

He leaned forward, dropped a kiss on her waiting mouth and grinned. 'What do you think?'

''Jon and I decided that since neither

of you are in the least bit happy living apart we would have to do something to get you together so that you could sort out your problems. I know you think that Grey was having an affair, Abbie, but Jon says he wasn't — ''

'And how would Jon know?' Grey wondered idly, his arms sliding around her waist, pulling her back against him so that he could nuzzle her neck.

'Shh. 'Anyway, you seem to have had such good times at Ty Bach that I thought that was the best place for you to be. Jon agreed.''

'He had a choice?'

Abbie giggled. ''Talk to one another, take all the time you need. I'm staying with Jennie Blake and Jon has gone to stay with his mother for half-term, so sadly no passion *this time*, and you needn't worry about either of us. Much love, Polly and Jon.''

''Talk to one another . . . ' You were right, Abbie. She's a clever little minx,' Grey said.

'Mmm. She'll need to be when she

tries to explain to her mother just how I came to write off her car.'

'I'll sort out the insurance for her.'

'The sooner the better. The postman says the roads are passable.'

'In a hurry to leave, are you? Some assignment that just won't wait?' There was just the faintest tension in his voice, and she turned and slipped her arms about his neck.

'No, love. Nothing in the whole wide world that won't wait.'

'Then I don't think we should take any chances. Leave it a day or two . . . ' But as he began to kiss her it was her turn to tense.

'Grey! The bacon's burning.'

Without pausing in what he was doing, he reached behind her and pulled the pan from the hob.

\* \* \*

Margaret, deeply sun-tanned and equally flustered, whispered, 'Why on earth didn't you let me know, Abbie? I would have come back earlier.' She smiled at Grey as he closed the boot. 'He is gorgeous! And you look wonderful too. How did it happen?'

'Ask Polly,' she said, laughing. 'She's got a lot to tell you.'

Margaret turned to her daughter, frowning a little as she noticed the antique gold locket that hung at her throat — her reward from Grey for playing cupid. 'Has she been a nuisance?' she asked anxiously.

'No, she's been quite wonderful. She can come and stay any time she likes.' She hugged Polly and they exchanged a conspiratorial grin. 'And . . . er . . . I'll leave her to explain why you've got a new car.'

'What?' And, while Margaret was busy opening the garage door and exclaiming over the shiny up-to-date model lodged within, Abbie slipped into the passenger seat of the Mercedes beside Grey.

'Ready to go home?' he asked.

'I can't wait. I've got a new job lined up.'

'So soon? I thought . . . ' He gave a little shrug, then leaned forward and started the engine. Then he turned it off again. 'No, damn it! I will *not* be quiet. I don't want you to go rushing off all over the world. I want you at home. With me.'

Abbie slotted in her seat belt and then looked up at him through her long, dark lashes. 'Grey Lockwood, are you planning to be terribly masterful and forbid me to work?' she enquired softly.

'Why don't you try me?' he growled.

'I'm almost tempted,' she replied, then, as his eyes gleamed dangerously, she held up her hands in mock surrender. 'Only kidding, my love. I promise. Actually, I'm going to be working from home — that's why I'm so eager to get back into a routine. Secret lunchtime trysts are a lot of fun, but this new project needs my full attention.'

'I see.' Slightly mollified, he restarted the engine. 'When were you planning to start this new project?'

'Mmm? Oh, it's already under way.'

'Already? When did this — ?' He stopped himself. 'Look, can't you put it on hold? I wanted to take you away. Somewhere warm, just the two of us.'

'Oh, I'd like that.'

'You're sure it won't interfere with your new *project*?' he asked, just a little tetchily.

'Oh, no, it'll be quite perfect. I can arrange for the decorator to be in while we're away.'

'Decorator!' He threw a startled glance at her.

'Yes. I'm going to need a special room, you see. I thought the study would be best, since it's next door to the bathroom. It will be easiest for the plumbing.' He didn't answer, and she leaned forward to look into his face. 'You don't seem very interested in my new venture. It's really very exciting.'

'I'm capable of providing all the excitement you can handle.' Then he added, with a lift of one shoulder, 'You should have discussed it with me first. We always used to discuss things.'

'I had intended to, but this just sort of cropped up . . . quite unexpectedly.'

'I see. Do you want me to do anything? Apart from evacuate the study, that is?'

Abbie smiled serenely. 'I think you've done everything you can for now, love, but I will need your help from time to time during the next few months — on a fairly regular basis. Don't worry, I'll give you plenty of notice. Then it's just a question of holding my hand, giving me some support during the crucial period. I don't want you disappearing on some . . . um . . . case conference at the vital moment.'

Her mischievous smile robbed the words of their sting, but nevertheless his dark brows drew into the slightest frown. 'I imagine you're going to need some finance. Plumbing can be expensive. And the kind of equipment you'll need for a darkroom.'

'Darkroom?' Her grey eyes danced. 'Whatever gave you the idea I was going to build a darkroom?'

'You're a photographer — what else . . . ?' He pulled into the kerb and turned to her. 'Tell me, Abbie, does this project of yours have any particular time-scale?'

She dropped her lashes demurely. 'Well, the initial production period is about nine months. After that it's . . . well, I suppose it's a lifetime.'

There was a moment's silence, then he reached across and took her hands. He was trembling and she clasped his fingers to steady them. 'You're having my baby?' he breathed. 'Are you certain? I mean . . . Oh, dear God, I don't know what I mean.'

'You don't mind? Last time we talked about it you weren't exactly enthusiastic. In fact, you were really rather angry about the whole thing.'

'Oh, my love. When you said that you wanted to start a family I had one moment of utter joy and then agony, as I realised that it couldn't happen — not then. That was why I was so angry. I was angry with Robert and Susan and

Emma. Most of all I was angry with myself, for getting involved in all their stupid deceptions.'

He stared down at their interlocked fingers. 'And then, when you seemed to be treating the whole thing as something to be got over with so that you could carry on with your career . . . I was angry with you.' He looked up. 'I was wrong, wasn't I? Completely wrong.' He released his seat belt and hers and put his hand very gently on her waist. 'He's there. A life we've made together. Abbie and Grey Lockwood made into a new person.'

'You're sure it's going to be a boy?' she teased.

'It doesn't matter.' He took her into his arms and held her. 'Abbie, I don't know what to say — how to tell you how much I love you. You are so beautiful, so good, so generous in your love that I can hardly believe that you're mine. I'll always be there for you,' he said, suddenly fierce. 'Always.'

She took his face in her hands and

kissed him, very gently. 'I think we should continue this conversation at home. We seem to have an audience.'

He looked around, saw three small boys staring at them from across the road and turned back to her with a grin. 'They're not interested in us, love. They're just looking at the car.'

'Are you sure?'

'Trust me,' he said. Then, as the darkness in his eyes intensified, Abbie sensed that he was no longer talking about the small boys. He was asking her to trust him for the rest of their lives.

'With all my heart, Grey,' Abbie murmured softly. 'With my life itself.'

Then, with a soft groan, Grey Lockwood took his wife into his arms and, mindless of their small audience, he kissed her.

## THE END

We do hope that you have enjoyed reading this large print book.

Did you know that all of our titles are available for purchase?

We publish a wide range of high quality large print books including:
**Romances, Mysteries, Classics**
**General Fiction**
**Non Fiction and Westerns**

Special interest titles available in large print are:
**The Little Oxford Dictionary**
**Music Book, Song Book**
**Hymn Book, Service Book**

Also available from us courtesy of Oxford University Press:
**Young Readers' Dictionary**
**(large print edition)**
**Young Readers' Thesaurus**
**(large print edition)**

For further information or a free brochure, please contact us at:
**Ulverscroft Large Print Books Ltd.,**
**The Green, Bradgate Road, Anstey,**
**Leicester, LE7 7FU, England.**
**Tel:** (00 44) 0116 236 4325
**Fax:** (00 44) 0116 234 0205

# THE SECRET OF THE SILVER LOCKET

## Jill Barry

Orphan Grace Walker will come of age in 1925, having spent years as companion to the daughter of an aristocratic family. Grace believes her origins are humble, but as her birthday approaches, an encounter with young American professor Harry Gresham offers the chance of love and a new life. What could possibly prevent her from seizing happiness? A silver locket holds a vital clue, and a letter left by Grace's late mother reveals shocking news. Only Harry can piece the puzzle together . . .